Bob Becomes an Agent

Bad Luck Bob
Book 1

P.J. Cruz

This is a work of fiction. Names, characters, business, events and incidents are the products of the author's imagination. Any resemblance to actual persons, living or dead, or actual events is purely coincidental.

Copyright © 2023 by Pj Cruz

All rights reserved.

No part of this book may be reproduced in any form or by any electronic or mechanical means, including information storage and retrieval systems, without written permission from the author, except for the use of brief quotations in a book review.

Image source: www.freepik.com. This cover has been designed using assets from Freepik.com

Cover design: Vinegarice

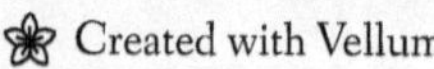 Created with Vellum

Thank you to all the people that helped me get to this point.

A special thank you to the first person to read and listen to my stories even when they were illegible scribbles on notebook paper in a Digimon binder.

Chapter One

The alarm blared. Bob sighed and drowsily tapped snooze on his alarm clock, which read 6:00 a.m. in bright red text.

He had about ten minutes of wiggle room but got up anyway. He tricked himself with that line way too many times and couldn't afford to be late today. After rolling out of bed and quickly stretching, Bob headed over to the bathroom of his studio apartment.

One of the few perks of living in a studio apartment was that he could leave everything where he wanted, including his gym equipment. He left his weights in front of the TV, a grip strengthener on his desk, and a medicine ball underneath the kitchen table. It was perfect. He didn't have anyone rearranging everything to make it better. The other perk was that it was just about the only thing affordable for the average 25-year-old in this city. His old place was better. Two bedrooms. Tons of amenities. Unfortunately, it required him to do a job that drained his soul. So, when he left it, he had to downsize. Bob tried the roommate thing, but it grew old faster than moldy bread, so he was stuck with a studio.

Bob's phone rang, playing the custom ringtone he set for his mom. He danced for the first few rings then spit out his toothpaste and answered.

"Hey, Mom."

"Hey, honey. Just wanted to make sure you were up," she said.

"Yup, yeah. I'm just getting ready."

"You know your father didn't think we should drive you? Can you believe that?"

"Oh, no, I agree. Mom, I say this from a place of love, but I can get myself to the shoot."

"I know, I know, but a mother never stops worrying."

"Yup. Love you too."

Bob's mom ran through her obligatory checklist of things to make sure he was ready, including whether he packed his lunch, ironed his clothes, and bought a present to give to the casting directors. After each question, Bob replied yes, though he sounded more annoyed each time.

Bob said, "You know we don't have to do this every time. I'm an adult."

"I don't care how old you are. I'm still your mother. Now, where did I leave off?"

She continued the questions like an interrogation. Once Bob survived that gauntlet, his mom enunciated a kiss and hung up. He smiled. She was the best, even if she was over-protective.

Bob looked back at his phone and sprinted for the door. No time for breakfast.

The city subway took him to Central Station, the meeting point for the shoot. The casting director, who worked for a studio he never heard of, included him on an email chain that told everyone where to meet. It was a little strange to not meet at the set or the studio, but Bob's friend swore it was legit, even though he had to dig the email out of his spam folder. She was waiting for him right outside the turnstiles that opened up into the main station.

Underneath a heavy indigo jacket, she wore her typical dark green ratty sweatshirt back from her college lacrosse days, though it was a bit tighter now that she wasn't training six days a week. Her hood was thrown back, catching some of her shoulder-length braids, the rest of which framed her oval face.

"Bro, you gotta believe me," she said. "Granted, they're a little weird, but they pay you, they feed you, and if you're good, they give you a callback on another project. The shows never hit, but my agent said it's great exposure."

"Moni, your agent is your cousin, and he's high ninety-nine percent of the time."

Moni rolled her eyes and kept eating her to-go muffin.

"You're just jealous that I have representation."

"I swear I'm not. You mind coming with me? I wanna grab a snack. I couldn't eat before I left."

Moni pulled out her phone after she finished the last bite of her muffin, which was a nauseating accomplishment. The entire station was underground—the perfect place for a dirty metallic smell to stew. The wall-mounted fans spun but didn't do anything to help the stench.

"Ah, sorry, bud. No can do," she said. "We're supposed to meet the bus in a minute." Bob frowned. She was right. Every place was either closed or had a line of twenty people. His stomach grumbled in protest. Empty stomachs and bus rides never well for him.

"You said they have food at these things?"

Moni nodded.

"Okay, fine. Let's head up."

The two puttered along on the escalator up to street level. Bob's nose patiently waited for the relatively fresh air to embrace his nostrils. Moni tugged on his sleeve.

"Hey, is that Charlie?"

"Seriously? Ned's brother? No way. I haven't seen him in months."

The terminal was a sea of commuters, tourists, and homeless people weaving through each other with expert precision. Bob stood on his tiptoes but still didn't have any luck spotting his old friend.

"I don't see him...Wait! No...Maybe it wasn't him."

"Yeah...um...you should invite him out with us."

"Yeah, sure. He's a blast."

"That and...he's built like a brick house."

"Go for it, Moni. My mom was saying he got some huge promotion at work, so he might also be a good sugar daddy."

Moni grinned.

The bus was there at 7:00 a.m. sharp. It was a black, unlabeled school bus and a dark film covered the windows. The bus door opened with a hydraulic *psssshhh* that revealed the bus driver, who was his own mystery. He wore black sunglasses (even though it was cloudy) and rocked a black suit, white button-down, and a black tie. His head and face were cleanly shaven.

The crowd of extras waiting near the top of the escalator filtered over and formed a line. Bob was sixth in line with Moni behind him. There were all sorts of people around him. One, because it was Central City, and the most unique people came here, and two, they were a bunch of wannabe actors who wanted to show off their uniqueness.

"This guy looks intense," Moni whispered in his ear. Bob nodded. He thought about agreeing out loud, but the driver looked like a trained watchdog ready to pounce on any word. The other actors were also quiet and just stared at the driver.

"Are you all here for the...show audition?" the driver said. The first person in line nodded, and then the rest of the line followed.

"Can you speak up? It's kind of loud, and we can't hear you," someone said from the back. Bob turned back. The speaker wore a bright pink polo shirt, Bermuda shorts, and a Bluetooth earpiece. The guy continued and said, "If you're here for the show extras, can you let us on? I don't want to be late."

The bus driver's hand crept to his waistband like he was going to draw a gun, then he jerked his hand away and grumbled to himself. With a yell, he said, "This is for the show extras. Was that loud enough for you in the back?"

The line giggled and replied yes.

"Okay, good. There are no assigned seats. Don't be a jerk and take up two seats. Your bags aren't that important. Put them on the ground. No, not that ground! On the ground in front of your seat." His gaze didn't leave Pink Polo Guy. "Did I make myself clear? Okay, good. Now, get on."

Chapter Two

Bob and Moni grabbed seats together right around the middle of the bus, which had two-by-two rows going all the way to the back. The inside looked like a charter bus with cloth seats fitted with a weird funky pattern like it was straight from the 1970s. They were moderately comfortable and quite conducive to napping.

"My cousin says always take the middle. That way, we aren't like too eager and can learn from the people in front of us, but, like, we also aren't looking like slackers like the ones in the back," Moni said.

Bob leaned his head against the window and glanced at Moni. "You said this was a comedy? This driver seems a little intense."

"Psh, forget about him. He's just driving there. My cousin swore this was a comedy."

"You mean your agent? Was he high when he told you this?"

"I was high. He might've been. Nah, he was working, so he was definitely sober."

"So, there's a chance you might've misheard him."

"A small chance." Moni pinched her fingers together for emphasis. "Why do you care, though? You did all those fitness classes."

"I'm going for the hot funny guy. Ryan Reynolds. Chris Pratt."

"Best of luck, dude, but you might be aiming too—hey, you feeling okay?"

Bob pursed his lips and turned to stare out the window. Moni kept talking to him, but he started feeling ill. He reached up to the ceiling vent and struggled to angle it into his face. Then Bob closed his eyes and focused on the vent blowing on his face.

"Nope," Bob said. "Going to focus on not throwing up."

Moni nodded and scrolled through her phone. "Oh, TRID's got some promotion going on later. We gotta—right, sorry, I'll leave you alone."

Bob did his best to focus on feeling better. He imagined he was back in his treehouse, his Super Scouts blanket over his head while he read a bunch of knock-off comic books. However, Pink Polo Guy's arrogant, entitled voice kept intruding.

"Yeah...yeah...yeah...yeah, I hear you. Just make sure I'm first on the list, okay? ...What do I pay you for? ...Okay, fine, technically my dad pays, but what is he paying you for?"

Bob's mind wandered to quiet conversations between other extras. They shared tips and practiced lines. Should Bob be doing that? They were just extras so he didn't expect to get lines, but what if the director asked him to star in another episode because he did so well? He smirked.

The bus ride smoothed out. Bob peeked to see where they were, but immediately felt sick and shut his eyes. Moni patted his thigh.

"We're out of the city, so things should be less jerky. Let me know if I need to get you a bag or something."

Bob slept for the rest of the ride. He didn't wake up until the brakes squeaked and the bus lurched forward. Moni tapped him on the chest.

"Wakey, wakey," she said.

Bob yawned. He looked out the window and thought they had time traveled. The buildings were an old Wild West design and shambled together with an old-timey saloon in the center. Two crossing dirt streets made the town layout look like a giant "X" with buildings on both sides of the street. Some other people, dressed like the bus driver, threw tumbleweeds out from second-story windows. One tumbleweed rolled along the street into a poorly disguised speaker that was likely the source of the vulture caws and desert whistle.

"Okay, I'm gonna ask you again, Moni," Bob said. "This is a comedy?"

Moni bit her lip. "I might've been really out of it."

Right as the last extra stepped off the bus, the doors slammed shut and the lock clicked.

"Welcome. Thank you all for coming," someone said. Bob jumped and turned to face the speaker. The person had long brown hair tied in a ponytail. He wore a bright yellow, loose fishing shirt and cargo pants with pockets so filled they looked ready to burst. His toes stuck out of his Velcro sandals.

"My name is Director McCarthy, and I'm going to be assigning your roles. As a disclaimer, this—" he glanced down at his clipboard— "show...is confidential and has a lot of security measures. Don't go looking in locked rooms. If you do, we will consider it treason." Director McCarthy enunciated treason and scanned the crowd. "This also has very realistic special effects, so if you see or hear a gunshot, we promise it's fake. If you hear a person screaming in pain, they are just superb actors."

Director McCarthy asked everyone to line up one by one. He checked their names against his clipboard, then pointed them in one direction or another. It was a little weird that they were checking to see no one snuck on now and not when the bus driver picked them up.

"Okay, you go to the saloon," Director McCarthy said. "You go to the haberdashery...It's a hat store, you idiot. Okay, saloon. You go to the ammo store."

Pink Polo Guy chimed in from deeper in the line. He said, "You mean the ammunition depot? I've trained in Westerns, so I feel like I could—"

"You could shut up. Actually, hang on. I misread. You," Director McCarthy said, pointing to Pink Polo Guy, "you go to the latrine." He pulled a pencil out of one of his pockets, erased something on his clipboard, then wrote *latrine*. He put the pencil back in a different pocket and pulled a two-foot-long beef jerky stick out of a different pocket no more than four inches tall.

"Hey, you," he said. Bob snapped up and realized he was up in line. "Robert Johnson, is it?"

"Yeah, I go by Bob, though."

"Got it. Okay, Bob, you're going to the jailhouse."

Bob nodded and headed over. Moni was waiting for him in the center of the western town. She had already changed into her costume. Moni wore a brown leather suspenders dress with a white blouse underneath, which contrasted with her dark complexion. Her black hair was still braided into dozens of strands with light brown highlights toward the bottom.

"What do you think? Should I ask to take it home?" she said, twirling around. Her outfit danced from side to side.

"I admit you kind of rock it. Don't think it fits your vibe, though," Bob said.

"Yeah, that's fine. I'm just happy they didn't say I was playing a 'slave.' I saw the western theme and got a little nervous. These guys seem okay, though." She punched him playfully on the arm. "See? Told you it's gonna be fine."

"Well, I'm in 'jail'," he said with air quotes.

"Rough. They put me in the saloon."

Bob gave a quick wave goodbye and headed to his assigned station to the east, surveying everything as he went. The rickety wooden buildings shook in the wind. Dust stained storefront windows so much that they were completely opaque. Ragtime music played to an uninterested crowd. Then Bob spotted more people in black suits, white shirts, black ties, and black shoes, just like the bus driver. The men were bald or had buzzcuts. The women had hair tied back in painful-looking buns or had short hair like Bob. They walked in and out of buildings, climbed into barrels on porches or in alleys, and zip-lined across the street between rooftops.

He reached into his pocket and texted his mom an update.

I'm still okay, but this place is a little weird.

Okay. Send me your location. If you don't answer in an hour, your dad and I will come get you, she responded, her overprotective parent voice echoing in Bob's head.

While drafting his response, Bob bumped into one of the suited people.

"Where are you supposed to be, sir?" she said. Her platinum blond hair was blinding, and her black sunglasses reflected the sun right into Bob's eyes.

"I'm heading to the jail. I was just texting my mom," he said.

"Okay, hurry along. We're beginning the operation—"

"The scene," said a man who spawned out of nowhere, dressed like the bus driver. "We are beginning the scene."

The woman nodded and said, "Ah, yes. The...scene. Of course. Yes. Okay. Well, move it."

Bob nodded, and the two black suit actors headed on their way. Bob texted his mom that he loved her, that he'd be fine, and she didn't have to worry so much. After putting his phone away, his phone vibrated again, but he didn't check it out because he already knew what his mom was going to say. They were always intensely protective.

Back in 7th grade, he told his parents that someone took his lunch money. He foolishly assumed they would talk to the principal and have a discussion with the bully's parents. Nope. They showed up the next day at recess in ski masks, armed with large soft drink cups, and dumped them on the bully. Then, they yelled, "Booyah!", said not to mess with Bob Johnson and escaped in their lime-green pickup truck with the license plate *JhnsnFam*. The bully didn't mess with him again, but the school also banned his parents from ever stepping onto campus again.

Bob headed up the jail's porch stairs, the wooden steps creaking under his weight. The building had a crudely painted sign over twin swinging doors and two people in black suits, one male and one female, on either side. They each had a finger to their earpieces and were mumbling something. It didn't look like they were conversing since they faced opposite directions, but they sounded like they were responding to each other. Neither of them looked at Bob as he pushed through the doors and made his way inside.

"Hi, I'm here for the jail. I'm one of the extras," he said. As his eyes adjusted to the dim jail, Bob recognized some of the extras from the bus. They wore orange and black striped jumpsuits with half wearing matching hats. They gathered toward the front of the open room near a cluttered bulletin board hosting dozens of wanted posters. Past them were three jail cells along the back wall and a closed office with a fogged glass pane. On the office door was a handwritten sign that said, *Don't come in. Secret.*

Bob wandered over to the bulletin board. The posters were mugshots on yellowed paper with frayed, curling edges. Most of the names were funny. Dr. Dirt. Sinister Stain. The Ominous Odor. They all looked like rejected supervillains with wacky hair and an absurd amount of makeup—except for one who looked normal. In fact, the person looked really familiar.

Before Bob could read the name, someone tapped him on the shoulder. Bob instinctively turned to see a round-faced woman with a ring of flowers in her hair. She wore a bright pink floral dress and tattoos of flowers wrapped around her arm, making it look like a candy cane.

"Oh, hi! It's so nice to meet you," she said. "My name is Linda McCarthy."

"Are you related to Director McCarthy?" Bob said.

"Yes, Director is my husband. Isn't he the dreamiest?" She clasped her hands and fluttered her eyelids.

"Yeah! He was super nice. I also wanted to say that I'm super excited to be here. If you have any feedback, I'd really appreciate it. I really want to get into acting."

"Oh, why, yes, of course. We love enthusiasm here, and it will really get you far," she said. Linda leaned in closer and whispered in Bob's ear. "If you want to get a bit farther,

Director and I offer...private lessons in our home." Then she squeezed Bob's arm and giggled.

Bob yanked himself back and retreated another step for good measure. "Okay, well, thank you for that," he said. A chill ran down his spine. "And sorry if I missed it, but what's your husband's name?"

"Director," she said. She took a step forward, and Bob took a step back. After giving a flirtatious wink, she pointed to the office. "Knock twice and say, 'Prisoner Three.' Actor Gilefski will provide you with your outfit, and you can change in the bathrooms out back."

It was a little strange for actors to do the behind-the-scenes work. It must be a low-budget show. Too eager to leave and not curious enough to think about it more, Bob dashed for a uniform, and then ran out to change. Once Bob rounded the corner, he spotted Pink Polo Guy randomly digging holes and making the ground look like a giant piece of Swiss cheese. There was also a black suit individual pointing at a new spot without looking and saying "dig" once Pink Polo Guy finished one. They both regarded Bob, then returned to their work. Bob worried he'd also be required to do hard labor.

He reported back to the jail to see most of the actors behind bars. Linda flashed a smirk, whipped out a megaphone, and started addressing them through it.

"Bob," she said, "we're getting in place. Hop into the cell."

The jail was way too small for a megaphone, and her voice bounced off the walls, making it way louder than it needed to be. Bob rubbed his ears while closing his cell door and scootching into the crowded space inside.

"Hey, man," someone whispered. "Do you have any tricks? This is my first time on a set."

The guy was a little shorter than him, with brown hair, facial hair, and chest hair. He wore the black and orange jumpsuit and a pair of glasses.

"Yeah," Bob said, "Well, not for Westerns specifically. Also, my friend said this was a comedy, but I'm starting to have my doubts. The actors are super serious—"

"Quiet!" Linda said through the megaphone.

"Just listen for your cue, and you'll do great," Bob said quietly to the person behind him.

"Action!" Linda said.

The office door swung open with a loud thud. Two people in suits stormed out with very realistic-looking guns. They had the word "actor" sewn into the back of their suits. They were so cool. Imagine making it so big that people could recognize who you were just by your movements and acting ability. Honestly, Bob didn't know who they were, but they must've been famous. He pinched himself for getting distracted. The number one thing his mentors said was "stay in character." Breaking character was the best way to get kicked off a set and not be invited back.

The two actors stopped at the swinging doors and took cover on the right side. They mumbled something to each other, then the one closest to the doors slowly pressed it out with her hand. She kept inching and inching until—

Bang! It was the most realistic sound effect Bob had ever heard. He had never heard a real gun in person, but it sounded like a super loud version of the ones that went off around his apartment.

Everyone in the cells shrieked and dropped to the floor. Linda didn't flinch.

"Prisoners! Need you up in your cells. I promise this is just all really good special effects."

Bob looked at the bullet-sized hole in the floor by her

foot and was very slow to stand up. The two actors rolled underneath the saloon doors and started firing. The shots' echo stretched for miles.

"I've been hit!" one of them said. Bob was more scared that he couldn't see what was going on.

"Agent—I mean actor! Actor down," the other said. "Seeking evac!"

Bob looked at Linda, who was casually flipping through papers on her clipboard.

"Mrs. McCarthy," Bob said, "do you think they need help? That one actor sounds pretty hurt."

She didn't look up. "Oh, they're fine. They're trained for action and combat. You know, the fake kind of combat." Then she looked up. "But please, call me Linda."

Another extra from the second cell said, "Linda, do you want us to do anything special?"

"Nope, you just stay in your cell. But please, call me Mrs. McCarthy."

Bob shuddered under the jealous gazes of the other extras. He wasn't imagining it because what they murmured amongst each other was mean. It wasn't like he wanted the special treatment. He was here to act just like everyone else.

The fighting outside got worse. At one point, Bob thought he heard a chainsaw, a sword sliding out of its sheath with a metallic whoosh, and monkeys shrieking. The whole time, Linda didn't look up from her clipboard. After minutes of standing around, she raised her hand and started counting down. Three fingers. Two fingers. One finger. The cell bars swung open automatically.

"Okay, everyone, proceed outside. If you feel any pain, that's just our state-of-the-art mental special effects. It makes your acting more realistic. Nothing permanent. Now break a leg," Linda said. She whirled her finger and pointed outside with the clipboard in the other hand. She wasn't too convincing, but then again, she was a professional. Maybe they really had mental special effects. Even if they didn't, he had to do well so he could use them as a reference for acting gigs. He gulped and hoped she was telling the truth.

Bob was the first out of his cell and gestured for the people behind him to follow, which they did reluctantly. He crept to the door, and when his foot stepped into the light casting past the swinging doors, a bullet crashed through the floor inches from his toes, scattering splinters around it.

"Ah!" he said and hopped backward. Bob felt someone slap his butt and shout.

"Go get them, tiger," that someone said. Without a doubt, he knew it was Linda. After easily choosing between the bullet and spending more time near her, Bob ran outside and threw his hands up.

"Please don't shoot me," he said. His heart raced. Sweat beaded along his hairline, and his stomach spun in ten different directions. Then Bob lowered his hands and raised his eyebrows. All the strange noises he heard and scenes he imagined were there. There were at least a hundred black suit actors between the street, the rooftops, and the sky. The ones in the sky wore jet packs or swung on ropes between buildings. Bob's jaw dropped.

A furry hand pushed up on his jaw, and Bob absently closed it, his gaze fixed on the tiny gorilla smiling up at him. His jaw wanted to drop again, but he held shut. The gorilla patted him on the stomach and then took a few steps back and winked.

Then the gorilla said in a regal voice, "Please stay in character. It's very helpful for this exercise." Bob almost didn't register what the gorilla said. After all, since when could gorillas talk? It had to be someone else, but the gorilla nodded and raised an eyebrow like it was making sure Bob understood.

Bob nodded at the gorilla then shook himself to get back into character. "You'll never catch me alive, coppers!" he said. He started running, and for a few moments, no one seemed to react. Linda didn't blare anything on the megaphone, his fellow extras didn't move or say anything, and the black suit actors just stayed in place. Even the flying ones.

He might've been doing the wrong thing. Linda didn't give great direction, and some person in a lifelike gorilla suit told him to stay in character. After all his blunders, he completely botched the whole sequence and was going to get fired. No doubt people would talk, and he'd get blocked from any more auditions. His acting career was over before it started.

"Get him! Don't let the prisoner escape," someone said, ringing the starting bell for all hell to break loose. Explosions in a melodic cadence sent heat washing over Bob like warm waves coming from seven different directions. The swords clanged, the bullets popped, and the gorillas roared. A building toppled onto another, and a witch's cackle pierced the sky. Bob didn't stop for any of it. He wanted to be an actor. He trained for months between acting and stunt classes and lifted weights 24/7. He wasn't stopping for anyone.

Then someone on horseback scooped him up, tied up his hands and feet with rope, and plopped him stomach-down on the horse's rear. However, Bob didn't realize until the third gallop and the manure smell from the horse's butt hit his nose. He craned his neck back and saw his captor was the platinum blond-haired actress he ran into earlier.

Bob stared down at the hard and unforgiving dirt below

and wondered how bad it would hurt to fall onto it. His attention moved up as the stampede of ravenous black suit actors chased after him after like an army of feral tigers.

"Actor Sol seized Prisoner 86!" one of them said.

Bob's gaze went back to the dirt, and he felt ill. They were going fast, and his still-empty stomach was not happy about it. Bob wobbled and closed his eyes.

"Hey, uh, miss, or ma'am, or I'm really sorry. I have really bad motion sickness, and we're going fast, and I thought this was a comedy, and I'm really trying, and I don't feel well, but I really wanted to pull this off, but maybe can someone else do this scene?" Bob said. Vomit leaped into his throat, but he pushed it back down. He closed his eyes and tried to remember his happy place.

For a second, he was mentally back in his treehouse underneath his Super Scouts blanket. His captor, Actor Sol, was under the blanket with him. She was sort of pretty. She had a heart-shaped face, a cute nose and a gorgeous smile. Her glasses covered her eyes, but they had to be gorgeous. Unfortunately, gorillas swung into the treehouse, ripped off the blanket, and smashed all the treehouse furniture he and his mom built. His happy place was short-lived.

Thud. Bob fell to the dirt and rolled. He brushed the dirt from his eyes just in time to see Actor Sol's hair bun release, letting her hair reach out in every direction. The sun hovered perfectly behind her head like a halo. Combined with the reflective sheen of her hair, it covered her in an ethereal glow. The horse turned and reared with pure majesty, and time seemed to slow. Butterflies fluttered in his stomach. She was probably famous and would turn him down, but all he could think about was asking her out.

Actor Sol reached out a hand and said something Bob

couldn't hear over all the chaos behind him. But he extended his own hand toward hers.

Right before they could reach each other, another black suit actor swung in on a rope tied to what looked like the sky and snatched Bob. In the next instant, they were sailing through the air like damn superheroes.

"Prisoner 86 secured," the actor said, his finger pressed against his earpiece. Bob did not feel secured. The black suit actor had grabbed him by the rope tied around his ankles, and he swung upside down about two stories off the ground and climbing higher. As the blood rushed to his head, Bob wanted to scream and cry. However, he wanted to be an actor more, so he kept quiet and stayed in character, which at this point only consisted of looking angry. The rest of his brain power remained focused on keeping what little was left in his stomach in place.

Bob squeezed his eyes shut, took deep breaths, and tried to block out what was going on. He told himself he wasn't moving. He imagined he was calmly sitting in his studio apartment with a really strong fan on his face. Things were going great until he suddenly became weightless.

When Bob opened his eyes, he was sailing through the air. By himself. Nothing keeping him from falling. The black suit actor that had swiped him was about twenty yards back at this point.

"This isn't a comedy!" he said. Below him, the other prisoners were in similar situations. Even the saloon had gun smoke wafting out of the windows in big billowy clouds. He hoped Moni was okay.

At last gravity took hold of him and heaved. The ground rushed up to meet him. "Ah!" he screamed, flailing his arms around. Maybe he could fly. Bob never tried before, but what better time to learn?

Right before he hit the ground, he landed in the arms of the platinum-blond actress on the same horse. He'd recognize her black sunglasses, black suit and tie, and white dress shirt anywhere.

"Oh, my God, thank you, thank you, thank you," Bob said. He started weeping, snot blasting out of his nose. Actor Sol's gaze was straight ahead, her stone-carved face showing an unwavering resolve. She dropped Bob onto the saddle uncomfortably squished between the saddle horn and her. Actor Sol reached for the reins with one hand and her prop gun with the other.

Bang! Bang! She fired, and two people howled. He closed his eyes and held on for dear life. The platinum-blond actress kept firing her prop gun as she made a sharp left turn. The horse slowed then stopped.

"Hey," she said. "Open your eyes." Bob felt her tap on his back. "You said you wanted out, right? Come on, off the horse."

Bob slid backward until his feet plopped onto the dusty ground, after which the woman cut his rope bindings. They stood in some alley about five feet wide and thirty yards long. In one direction was the chaos of the scene, and behind them was a desert stretching for miles, not a tree in sight. Actor Sol tied her hair back and growled.

"Damn Agent Myers. He always knows my hair gets in the way," she said.

"Did you say agent?" Bob said.

"No, I said...Actor." Her tone flicked up at the end, making it sound like she was asking Bob.

"Oh...okay..." He gulped.

"Yup. So, are you feeling okay? My cousin gets bad motion sickness." She finished tying her hair back.

"Yeah, I, uh, just need some time to, you know, sit and relax."

"Of course. You'll be safe here, so just hang out until Director and Linda shout cut."

"Thank you." Bob investigated the area by looking up and peeking into some nearby barrels. No one was around. "So, what kind of production is this?"

"What kind of production do you think it is?"

"A comedy?"

"Yup, that's exactly what it is," she said and gestured all around. "Nothing funnier than a western backdrop. It's really up-and-coming. We think *this* is the movie that's going to get picked up."

"I thought this was a show," Bob said.

"Yeah, that's what I said. What do you think I said?" She added prop bullets into her prop gun.

"I guess I'm still feeling woozy. Are we in danger?" Bob said, leaning forward. The platinum-blond actress shrugged her shoulders, but Bob couldn't take his eyes off the barrel of her gun. For a second, it pointed right at him. He took a step back toward the desert.

"Danger? No! I'm sure you're fine. Like I said, just hang here and—" She reached up to her earpiece and mumbled. She turned away, and Bob couldn't decipher what she said. It sounded like Latin. Once her private conversation stopped, Bob knew it was his chance. He took a deep breath and said a silent prayer.

"Hey, do you want to—"

"Hold that thought. I gotta get back into place, but if you make it to the next filming, ask me then." With that, Actor Sol ran back into the chaos, guns blazing.

Bob sighed in defeat and fell back against the building. He slid down like a slug and sat on the ground. The jail outfit was pretty comfy and had some butt cushioning that he really appreciated. While he had time to pass, he took out his phone and checked all his notifications. A few of his friends texted him about going out tonight, and after the day he had, he really could use some fun.

I'm in, he wrote. There was one response after another. *Yeah!* and *Can't wait*. Bob smiled.

In fact, Bob was so enthralled on his phone that he didn't notice the helicopter flying overhead, the pack of attack dogs that were released into the scene, or the flamethrower that incinerated the building fronts.

Chapter Three

"Cut!" Director McCarthy said over the megaphone. "Everyone meet in the town center for a wrap, and then we'll send everyone to the next scene. Great work on this...uh...comedy movie—television show."

Bob didn't love that there were more scenes, but he looked at his watch. They'd only been shooting for thirty minutes. That's showbiz, baby. Bob stood up and headed over.

The people in the town square were more outrageous looking than the ones lined up in the bus line this morning. The other prisoners had their uniforms singed or completely torn. Some extras had bruises all over their exposed skin, some sunburn, and some soot. Moni, who was now wearing dark blue jeans and a leather vest, had a series of ears on a necklace. Pink Polo Guy wore the same latrine digger costume, just covered in what looked and smelled like fecal matter.

"You all did a fantastic job," Director said, this time without the megaphone.

Linda smiled and clapped her hands. "Oh, yes. This went so well, and we got some really good footage. So, after you get some food, please head to your buses. It's very important that you go to the same bus that took you here."

"Thank you again, and we'll catch you on the flip side," Director said. He clapped his hands. Then he and Linda walked down one street, hand in hand, giggling with each other. Bob shivered when he thought he heard Linda say his name. It could've been for his performance, but Bob seriously doubted it.

The extras slowly dissipated, and Bob spotted Moni again.

"Wow, so what's happening with you?" he said. "I thought you were a saloon bar wench, now... You kill people?"

Moni flexed her arms then gestured at her ear necklace as they headed for a long white folding table covered in trays of delicious-smelling breakfast food.

Eggs, muffins, fruit, home fries, hashbrowns. It was like the "Mega Breakfast Mondays" Bob's dad prepared back when Bob was in middle school. His best friend and his brother would come over too. He'd have to ask how they were doing the next time they all went out.

"I prefer the term 'liberated the working class'. Not too shabby, though, huh? The American dream! But yeah, these guys were like 'give us the money,' but then I just smashed a bottle over one of their heads. He really sold it with the blood pack underneath the wig, and he didn't move, even after I kicked him. Then I convinced the other extras to stage an uprising, and we formed a gang."

"In," Bob said and checked his phone, "thirty minutes?"

"Thirty minutes! Really makes me wonder if teaching is my calling."

"I thought you said acting was your calling?"

"Yeah, that too. I can have multiple callings."

"Now you have a third one? Staging uprisings?" Bob pointed to her necklace then started grabbing food.

"Yeah, maybe. Oh, right, the necklace. So, Linda told me to just cut people's ears off and that they were prosthetics. Super realistic and stuff. Called my gang the 'Los Lobeos'. Isn't that cool?"

"Literally so cool," Bob said. "I just met this actress, got motion sickness, and then sat in an alley. There's no way I get cast again." He took a defeated bite of his food. He was bummed out, hungry but also nauseous at the same time.

"Nah, don't say that. And tell me more about this actress." She elbowed Bob. "She cute? Gonna be the next Mrs. Johnson?"

Bob blushed. "Yeah. I mean, I thought she was cute, but like, I don't know. She's way out of my league."

Moni laughed and slapped Bob on the back. After calling him hopeless, Bob went back to the jail to change into his old clothes while Moni went back to the saloon.

When Bob got back to the jail, he saw Actor Gilefski sitting in the back office with his feet propped up on the desk, chair leaned back, thumbing through some magazine. The actor didn't react until Bob knocked on the door.

"Oh wow. Bob, right? What are you doing here?"

"They want us to return our costumes? And I was hoping to get my clothes back." Bob was a little thrown off by the actor's surprise.

Actor Gilefski sighed and tossed his magazine onto the desk. He got up, clearly irritated by Bob's request, and combed through cluttered shelves along the office wall. After a minute of searching, he chuckled to himself.

"I forgot. They're gone."

"Um...What do you mean they're gone? Like, you're saying my clothes...are gone."

"Yeah. Totally slipped my mind. *Super* busy with actor stuff and all. You get it."

Bob gritted his teeth as the jerk continued.

"Yeah, so Linda called and said she accidentally grabbed them when she was getting the laundry from this scene."

"Well, can she come back? Am I supposed to just walk around in my boxers?"

"See, I tried calling her, but couldn't get a hold of her. I do need your costume. Well, um..." He returned to searching the cabinets and yanked out a dry-cleaning bag. "You can borrow these. Let me know if they fit."

Bob opened up the bag. There was a black suit and tie, just like what the other actors wore. Too annoyed to ask permission, he stormed back to the latrines, changed, then returned to see Actor Gilfeski lounging again, though he was a little startled when Bob returned.

"Ugh! Now—oh, it's you. Well, the suit fits well, I guess."

His lack of confidence gave Bob a bad feeling.

"You're sure it's okay I borrow this?"

"Yeah, it's probably fine. Just, like, make sure you get into the right bus line or...just make sure, alright?"

Actor Gilefski sat back in his chair and returned to his relaxed position. "Go on. Buses are leaving."

Bob stifled a tirade by biting his lip and walking out. After thanking himself for holding onto his phone, Bob imagined all the terrible things that might've happened if he left it in his clothes.

After getting laughed at by Moni, they headed over to the dozens of buses, each the same black school bus with tinted windows and sea of chatting extras surrounding them, making it hard to find a line. Fortunately, each bus was labeled with a different destination. Bob eyed what looked like the Central City one. Moni spotted some members of her gang and ran over to chat for a bit.

"Save me a seat," she said before the crowd swallowed her up. Bob ambled in the slow-moving line, and after what felt like forever, scrolled through his phone to see what was going on in the real world. Some celebrity drama, spicy court cases, and a bunch of group chats with funny pictures and videos. Someone told him he wasn't in the right line. After a quick thanks, he flipped over to one of his games and played that, and suddenly he was climbing the bus stairs. Bob had to finish the game before the bus got moving, so he couldn't take his eyes off it. He snagged a row and sat on the outside, leaving a space for Moni to sit next to him.

The seats were extremely comfortable. It must've been because he was so exhausted from the first scene that sitting was such a blessing. Bob finished the game and tucked his phone into his pocket. His head was heavy, then his eyelids were heavy. It couldn't hurt to clock out for a few minutes. Moni would spot him and tell him to slide over. Taking a nap would be fine.

When Bob woke up, he was in an empty and parked bus. The nap had worked wonders, and he was feeling immensely better. He wiped the drool from his face, gave a quick stretch, and got off the bus.

He was in a hangar with jets, tanks, and buses parked in rows throughout the gigantic space. At the far end were two massive, sliding metal doors large enough to cover a stadium. The walls and ceiling were concrete, and the floor was pavement, with various markings that looked like lanes. One lane led to his left, far from the hangar doors and deeper into the facility. The hangar ceiling slanted down and pointed to a normal-sized blue door. This next scene would likely take place in a secret government facility.

While heading to the door, Bob tried to flag down a couple of people walking around. They were busy unloading another bus's storage and told him that there was a meeting in the briefing room.

"Where? Sorry, this is my first day," Bob said.

"Oh, really, first day? Hey, Myers!" the guy said. He wore the same suits as the black suit actors, but no sunglasses, and his tie loosely hung around his neck. He had some cuts on his face, and a bit of blood stained his shirt. Bob couldn't tell if it was his or someone else's.

"Myers, this guy was one of us," he said laughing.

Myers popped out from behind a bus. He sort of looked familiar, wearing the same outfit, but Bob thought he might've been the person who swooped him on the zipline and threw him.

"Oh, wow! Really sorry for snagging you. If I knew you were one of us, I wouldn't have given you that hazing," Myers said, then laughed uncomfortably.

"Oh, you guys are extras too? I thought you guys were the actors. Oh, that? Yeah, no worries," he said. In the back of his head, Bob was terrified of going through that again. There were lots of worries. Innumerable worries.

Myers elbowed the first guy and said, "Oh, yeah, can you believe this guy? Yeah, we are *definitely* extras." He gave a wink. Bob nodded, but inside he was confused about the wink.

"So," he said, "I'll just follow this inside for the briefing?"

The first guy said, "Yeah," then gave Bob some extra directions. With a quick thanks, Bob made his way to the blue door. He walked quickly since he didn't want to be late. Who knows how long he slept on the bus? He was also a little annoyed that Moni didn't wake him up. She was usually good about that. Maybe someone took her spot.

After a couple of minutes, he reached the blue door with a large circular emblem with a red-filled and blue-outlined border. In the center of the logo, an eagle wore a patriotic chest piece and held a spray bottle in one talon, a toilet scrubber in the other. A green-back sponge stood proudly behind the eagle. Framed by the blue border, the initials C.L.E.A.N. encircled the emblem. Bob swung open the door and headed in.

The door opened into a foyer. Past it was a large room, the size of an auditorium. It looked like a NASA control center. Dozens of monitors hung along the back wall, serving as the room's focal point. Each monitor displayed a different laundromat feed. Bob watched people walk in and wait for their washing machine or dryer to finish. Their outfits ranged from tank tops and shorts to heavy winter coats, depending on the screen. Some feeds had signs in different languages.

The monitors towered over rows of computers where dozens of black-suited actors typed furiously. They popped up constantly and called back to a woman standing behind a podium about fifteen feet from Bob.

"Director Dawn," they'd say, then relay their message. She'd respond with a three-to-five-sentence answer, and they sat back down. The monitor then changed images and the process repeated. It was like a game of secret agent whack-a-mole.

To either side of the foyer were long blue hallways with white marble floors that looked identical. All Bob could think was that this show had a massive budget.

"Hi, excuse me," Bob said quietly to the woman behind the podium.

She raised her hand and rolled a sideways finger as a sign to tell Bob to keep talking.

"Yeah," Bob said, "I'm sorry to bother you. I promise I didn't—"

"Spit it out, agent."

"Wait, sorry, are we film—I'm so sorry for interrupting. Where should I go?"

"Briefing room. Right hall, fourth door, passcode 48231787, and password is 'hygienic'."

Bob quietly thanked her and slunk back toward the hallway. None of the hallways had signs and were rather generic. It didn't help that Bob had to navigate while straining to remember the passcode. He whispered it to himself so softly that the words barely left his lips. Bob felt bad enough for interrupting a scene. He wouldn't do it again.

The black suit actors he passed along the way didn't react to him. Some talked about things that fit within the context of the scene—missions, objectives and being undercover—but most went on about their weekend plans, upcoming vacations, or the new boat they bought. Bob wasn't sure if they were in scene or between scenes. There weren't any people with cameras or boom sticks. Bob spotted a few security cameras that might be used for filming, but he really hoped that wasn't the case in a big-budget production like this.

Unfortunately, Bob remembered the last scene didn't have any cameras either, but they said they got some good footage. This just might be the show's shooting style. Bob immediately straightened up to be safe.

For the last few seconds before he found the briefing

room door, which was labeled with a silver plaque right next to it, he repeated the passcode in his head.

The door had a plain oak glossy finish and a small silver monitor, roughly the size of a phone, and a keypad right above the door's handle. Bob mumbled the passcode to himself as he typed in the numbers. Then he whispered "hygienic" into the silver monitor. There were two clicks, and the keypad rotated to reveal a fingerprint scanner.

Bob pressed his thumb, but the silver monitor's screen turned red and beeped. Then the system reset. Bob typed in the passcode cautiously this time, accentuating each number and pressing down with much more confidence, as if trying to convince the keypad to let him in. Again, the two beeps sounded, and he tried another finger. He growled. After a fourth time, the door clicked open, but it revealed a black suit actor standing behind it.

"Sorry about that," she said quietly. "Must be acting up. Hurry up and sit in the back. Briefing's started."

Bob snuck to the back wall of the long, dark office. Six black suit actors, including the one who let him in, sat on either side of a wooden table, the projector in the center casting a presentation on the screen. All the actors stared attentively at the person presenting. Not one reacted to Bob entering.

"So, now that we know the locations that might be the next targets, it's important for us to coordinate with DHS and the CIA to make sure this is on their radars. Look, I get it. I know we're spread thin coordinating with Brazil and Egypt, but this is on our home turf. If C.L.E.A.N. needs to make a stand, it's here." The lights came back on, and the presentation vanished.

The speaker stood at the front of the room. He was an older-looking bald man with bushy white eyebrows and blue eyes. He had a muscular neck, and the rest of his muscles pushed up against his suit. Every time he turned, Bob thought he would tear the fabric.

"Any questions?" he said.

Bob raised his hand. "Yeah, hi, sorry. I'm Bob. I'm one of the extras," he said.

The old man chuckled. "Ah, *yes*. Very funny. Of course. What's your question, Bob?" he said.

"So, I get the goal. Stop the bad guys, but where do you need me?"

The old man's jaw dropped, and all the actors sitting around the dark wooden table turned to face Bob, their jaws similarly dropped. Bob thought his heart was going to leap out of his chest. Each gaze felt like a hundred degrees, making Bob sweat. Then the old man started clapping. Not one of those sarcastic claps, but a genuine good-job clap.

"Everyone, this is exactly what we need. Bob, you bring that energy to this next assignment," he said, wiping a tear from his eye. "As many of you know, this is my last mission as Director of C.L.E.A.N., and I always wonder about the future of the agency. But it's times like these"—he pointed at Bob— "where I know the agency is in good hands."

The rest of the actors joined in the clapping. All of them except one. Actor Sol. Bob's eyes went wide when he recognized her platinum-blond hair and the shape of her nose. Without her glasses, he barely realized who she was. Her face was a mix of confusion and conflict, like she was debating whether to call him out on some rumor she heard. Bob thought about all the black suits—the way they talked, the earpieces, the gadgets, people mixing up the words *agent* and *actor* or *operation* and *scene*, the fact that Moni might not have been on the same bus as him, all the danger he was in back at the western town, and how the black suit actors laughed when he said he was one of them. It all clicked. Bob was the secret.

His heart raced. This wasn't what he thought it was. Bob wasn't prepared at all. He was in way over his head. He wasn't an extra. Bob...was an actor now, and they were already filming the next scene.

Chapter Four

The clapping faded, and the black suit actors slowly stepped out of the room, some of whom struck up conversations about their personal lives. It sounded like the scene was over, but Bob never heard anyone say "cut." Actor Sol made a beeline to Bob, her hair elegantly bouncing with each step. He smiled. She had to have remembered that he wanted to ask her something.

Next filming, he thought. This was it. This was his time to ask her out. Actually, they were at work. His smile faded.

They were at work and mid-filming. Maybe. Bob would be such an ass to ask her now. Could he subtly float the idea? Potentially bring up that he was free Friday night and during the weekend? No, that was probably still wrong. He had to be respectful and professional. His heart pounded. Were they still filming? There was too much going on!

"You! Funny guy," the old man said, startling Bob. Actor Sol came to a quick halt, turned to the old man, and stood still, his words freezing her in place. Bob did the same but had a hidden feeling of disappointment that he lost a chance to talk to her. It was probably for the best since he was awful at small talk, especially when it was with someone he had a crush on. For now, he just hoped that he'd have a chance to hang out, stay on set, and have another chance to talk to her.

The old man continued and said, "How about you come with me, and we can chat in my office? I'll get you up to speed on the target."

"Oh, I think that she wanted to talk," Bob said, slowly turning his gaze to Actor Sol.

"Agent Sol? You guys can chat after. I'll be quick, then you can get back to it," the old man said.

Actor Sol nodded. "I agree, Director Veritably. I'll defer to you," she said.

Director? The words hung in the air. Bob wondered if it was a common first name in the film industry like some sort of speak-your-dreams-into-existence thing. Or was that his title for this production? They seemed calm and not acting like secret agents, so this was probably a break between scenes. Also, he called her Agent Sol and not Actor Sol. When did her title change? Maybe she also got a promotion. He'd play along for now.

"Perfect!" Director Veritably said and signaled Bob to follow along. But Bob didn't notice until Agent Sol cleared her throat a couple of times.

After the two left the briefing room, they turned so many times Bob thought they were in a maze. He tried to memorize the path from the motivational posters scattered around, which kept up with the cleaning vibe of everything else. One featured a deodorant stick with the caption, *Keep calm and roll on.*

"Right in here," Director Veritably said. He vanished into an office, and Bob followed him.

The muted green walls and the light wooden floors softened everything in the office. On the left-hand side of the office was an ornate and heavy desk where Director Veritably took his seat, and a wall of bookshelves filled with textbooks, trophies, and photos of people Bob didn't recognize. Across from that hung many different degrees so extensive that it blotted out all the wall's color. Master of Microbiology. Doctorate in Pathogenic Studies. Master's in Hygienic Engineering.

"Please take a seat. So, what's your name again?" Director Veritably said.

Bob tried to slide the chair back, but it snagged on a random flooring plank. He awkwardly slipped around the armrests, banged his knee on the desk, and sat.

"Bob. My name is Bob." He discretely rubbed his knee.

Director Veritably leaned back with his feet on the desk and interlocked fingers on his stomach.

"Bob. Short. Simple. Good name for around here. A lot of people here got some connections, or it's a generational thing. Their parents and grandparents worked here, so the youngins want to brag. I founded the damn place. Who do they think they're trying to impress?"

"Oh, yeah, this is my first time here. My parents weren't in the industry."

"See, that's refreshing. There's too much nepotism, and it leads to weak performers."

"Oh, no, that's not me. Well, actually, what do you like to see from your performers?"

"Initiative. Everything else can be trained. Initiative— like the stuff you showed in that meeting."

Bob smiled. Maybe he could have a career as an actor. Bob quit his career, got a part-time job, took acting and stunt lessons, and trained his body every day for the role. His parents were half supportive, half "why did you give up your secure and lucrative career." There were times that doubt screamed loudly in his head, but with one simple sentence everything turned bright. He impressed someone who looked confident, sounded important, and could be the production house director, a good connection in the industry. That's how you made it in showbiz.

Director Veritably chuckled. "Oh, don't let it get to your head. The main reason I brought you in was to discuss what's going on. Dirt is back." He put his feet on the floor, his face stern, his voice cold. The lights around the office dimmed, and a desk lamp flicked on. It suddenly felt like an interrogation.

Bob's eyes went wide. He had no idea what that was. It didn't come up in any of the acting classes he took or from any of his gym trainers. He thought back to all the emails he received for this gig. None of them had scripts or attachments or mentioned dirt. He memorized everything. Or maybe he didn't. Maybe someone accidentally forgot to include him on that email. Maybe he missed an email in his spam folder. Bob's face contorted with fear.

"Good," Director Veritably said. "I'm glad you appreciate the gravity of the situation."

"Yeah, I definitely understand what is happening right now. It might be helpful, though, to give some more background in case there is something I missed in my preparation." Bob prayed that Director Veritably did not notice he was improvising.

Director Veritably slammed a fist on the desk. Bob jumped in his seat, which Director Veritably didn't seem to notice.

"Where the hell have you been this whole time?"

Bob gulped. He pushed his luck too far. Then, his counterpart smiled.

"You make damn good points, and you leave nothing to chance. But in all seriousness, D.I.R.T., being the Dastardly International Rude Team, is bad news. I thought they were done, but Former Agent Lorox flipped and took the reins. He took critical information from C.L.E.A.N. and now knows that the United States' laundry industry is highly susceptible to attack."

Lorox was Ned's last name. What are the odds? He really should text him to catch up. Wait. The laundry industry?

Bob squinted and glanced around, trying to figure out if he was serious. This had to be a scene. Moni's cousin said this was a comedy. Good C.L.E.A.N. and evil D.I.R.T. It was ridiculous. On the other hand, this could be one of those action-comedy shows that were super popular when he was growing up. Director Veritably spoke with such venom in his voice that Bob couldn't imagine someone saying it with a straight face in real life. Bob had to act along.

"The...laundry industry?"

"Yeah, it's *that* bad. Laundromats have hundreds, if not thousands, of software vulnerabilities, and with the spike in smart washing machines and dryers in the home and at laundromats, hackers have opportunities to attack unprotected systems. The things they could do it's scary, Bob. The guys in the lab are working on anti-hacking software for these appliances, but we just haven't had enough time to develop and roll out the software. What's worse is that Americans are less trusting, so we couldn't install it even if we had it ready since the usual tricks don't work anymore."

"Yeah, those tricks being..." This had to be part of the show. This was the insane kind of stuff his conspiracy-theorist uncle wrote in his blog posts.

"My favorite was smart pizza boxes that wirelessly installed anti-virus software on vacuums, washing machines, and things like that. Then, once the upload was complete, people would throw out the pizza boxes and be none the wiser."

Bob's mind raced back to his apartment and the daunting stacks of pizza boxes. They were too wide to fit down the garbage shoot of his apartment, and the basement —where the recycling was—was a little scary, so the boxes stayed stacked in his apartment. He shivered. This script was hitting close to home.

"Oh, don't worry," Veritably said. "We stopped doing it. People got too wary of taking unordered pizza. DoorDash this, Uber Eats that. It's just getting too hard for this job. I feel like I'm stiffing you guys with the mess, but at least they have people like you to clean up."

Bob groaned. At first, because the hygiene puns were never-ending. After that, it was because this plot was complicated, and he had a hard time taking it seriously. Would anyone believe there was a top-secret hygiene war that involved world-ending proportions? How could people even relate to this story? But Veritably exuded fear and anger of a professional caliber. It's hard to believe that Bob was so unprepared to be an actor. He thought it was just getting in shape, memorizing lines, and getting auditions. Bob totally missed the part where the greats trained them- selves to believe that the plot was real. That had to be it. Veritably was one of the greats.

Bob mulled it over as Veritably explained that if a person could control the tones and timers on laundry machines, you could delay or speed up cycles so your shows wouldn't be interrupted, or you could make a dish- washer run extra loud during competing media, leaving the viewer with a distaste of it. Terrorists could control what people watched or even what they liked. Bob pretended to focus, but in his head he appreciated how lucky he was to meet Veritably. The man might be an excellent mentor.

There was a knock at the door and then it creaked open. Agent Dawn, the woman who stood in front of the podium in the big TV room, walked in. Her eyes were gray and thin, and her face sharper than Bob initially realized. The woman's dark hair hung neatly around her face, and the ends curled up right underneath her jawline. She wore the same blue dress and white jacket as before. Also, like all the other actors Bob had met, she was in incredible shape.

"Ah, Director Dawn," Director Veritably said, standing up. "Meet our newest recruit."

She closed the door behind her and regarded Bob with disappointment. She then rolled her eyes, extended a hand, and said, "Nice to meet you."

Bob did the same.

"Also, I want to clarify," she said, "that I'm not director until you retire."

"Oh, you care too much about formalities," Director Veritably said with a dismissive hand flick. "Well, since I have you, I was hoping you could take Bob to the training course. It's his first day."

She sighed, pulled out a phone from her pocket, and flipped through several screens. "That explains a lot. Unfortunately, I'm booked up, but it looks like Agent Sol is available. I'll assign her to be his mentor. She's one of my top agents."

"Perfect! Okay, Bob, Director—I mean Agent Dawn—and I have to chat. So please excuse us and meet Agent Sol in the briefing room," Veritably said. He must've noticed

Bob's confused face because he said, "The place where I gave that presentation."

Bob smiled and nodded. He also gave a nod to Agent Dawn, who didn't look his way. Afterward, Bob navigated his way back to the briefing room using the pictures along the walls as markers. Unfortunately, he got to the briefing room door, and his mind went blank trying to remember the passcode. Those stupid numbers! There were some in his head, but they swam around in random patterns in the mental soup of every number series he had to learn over the course of his life. He leaned, knocked on the door and whispered "Hygienic" into the slit between the door and frame.

Nothing changed. He tried a few times and eventually sat down. Bob couldn't tell whether they were filming or between scenes. There were no cameras or film crew. No script or an explanation of his character. His coaches mentioned that some directors really loved when their actors improvised, but Bob desperately needed parameters. He let out a sigh and leaned his head back, clunking against the wall with a defeated thump. He wondered how Moni was doing. She really kicked ass in the last scene, so she was probably fine. Bob wished she was here. She was great at listening.

Suddenly, the door clicked and opened. Someone cleared her voice and said, "48231787. If it helps, the code is a combination of the latitude and longitude of Paris, and the year bleach was invented. Bleach was invented in Paris. Just some fun C.L.E.A.N. trivia." Bob turned his head and saw Agent Sol standing in the doorway with her hair down and tie loosened.

Bob gave her a smile and scrambled to his feet.

"Oh, hi, Actor—Agent Sol. Yeah, that is super helpful. I'm good with lines, but numbers...not so much."

"So, you were really one of us the whole time? Had me fooled and I'm usually pretty sharp on this stuff."

"Yup. I mean, I didn't know either. I didn't even find out until I got here. Things just started moving and grooving, then I woke up in the facility. It's really just been keeping up at this point and I hope I'm doing well, but you never really know."

"You talk a lot when you get nervous, huh?" Agent Sol uncomfortably chuckled.

"My mentor recommended I work on that, but I haven't really had a chance. Well, I—"

"Okay, I'm gonna stop you there. Director Veritably told me to take you through the training course. He must have high hopes for you. Most newbies don't take that bad boy on until week 12."

Bob opened his mouth to say something but shut it before anything got out. Instead, he just gave a quick nod. Agent Sol smiled back.

"You learn quick..."

"Bob."

"You learn quick, Bob. Now, let's get to work."

Agent Sol took Bob to the unisex locker room and his own locker, where he had a dark blue T-shirt, white mesh shorts, and white sneakers waiting for him. Strangely and concerningly, every article of clothing was the perfect fit for him.

"My locker is around the corner, but we can meet back at the door. Then we'll head to the course and get back to it." Bob let out a sigh of relief. It sounded like they were taking a break from filming.

It wasn't until Bob saw Agent Sol in a T-shirt and athletic shorts that he realized how muscular she was. Her shoulder, arm, and leg muscles bulged through with clear definition. He checked out his own body, which was impressive in its own right. Bob trained for months and adjusted his diet, and the results showed. But she made him look like a novice.

"Okay, so, you ready?" she said. Bob gave her a thumbs up.

"So, what's the motivation for this next part? Where are there cameras and stuff?" he said.

"Cameras?" Agent Sol said, cocking her head to the side in confusion. "I mean, we have cameras running all the time. They got eyes watching us 24/7."

"Cool, cool, cool," Bob said. He pursed his lips together and gestured for Agent Sol to lead. When Agent Sol wasn't looking, he pressed his fingers to his temples and muffled a sigh. Bob literally found out he was an actor not even an hour ago. Now, he learned they were constantly filming. He thought he had breaks! He thought there would be someone to announce action or cut. To find out that this was a constant rolling scene was unsettling. There were so many instances where he felt he dropped character or didn't perform to the best of his ability. This wasn't acting—it was basically reality TV!

"Hey, you coming?" Agent Sol said. Bob glanced up to see there was a distance between them. He cleared his throat.

"Yeah, I just had to tie my shoe and stuff."

"So, I was just imagining you standing there and not moving?" she said, tapping next to her eye. "You managed to get who you were by me, but that's it. Now, I'm watching you like a hawk."

Agent Sol explained to Bob that he shouldn't expect to clear the obstacle course on his first try, though Veritably really wanted him to pull it off. The last person to do it on the first try was Agent Lorox. Her voice trailed off when she said the name. He couldn't wait to tell his friends that they had the same last name as the main villain.

They stopped in front of a pair of heavy, brown, and metal double doors. Agent Sol leaned in to push them, her back muscles bulging as she strained to get the door open. After several seconds, the doors budged enough that she could barely slip through, and they slammed shut behind her.

"Your turn," she said, the closed doors muffling her voice. Bob flexed his wrists, quickly stretched, and jogged in place. After a couple of hops, he ran full speed at the daunting door.

Bob expected some resistance. Instead, the doors immediately flung open like they were made of cardboard. The combination of all his momentum and no resistance sent him tumbling to the floor with Agent Sol standing above him with a smirk on her face.

"Sorry, I couldn't help myself. Rookie prank," she said, the smile never leaving her face. She helped Bob to his feet. He was annoyed, but once his eyes met hers, he couldn't help but return her smile. For a flash, she blushed then turned away. Bob blushed too. One, because he liked her. Two, because he might actually have a chance that she said yes to a date.

The room was dim, only illuminated from the overflowing hallway light. It smelled like stale sweat and looked like his high school gymnasium, but ten times the size. There was a click and then dozens of ceiling lights—metal tubes connected to wide, brown cones—buzzed on in an outward gust extending from where Bob stood. The walls were dark gray brick, the C.L.E.A.N. emblem prominently emblazoned on the walls to Bob's left and right. Either brown or rusted fans, Bob couldn't figure out which, spun in the ceiling corners, though he couldn't feel any of the breeze. The room also had glossy wooden floors that made his shoes squeak with each step.

The lights revealed the obstacle course in the center of the gymnasium. It was longer than a football field and built on an elevated surface supported by thick concrete pillars roughly fifteen feet high and ten feet apart. The course looked like a series of shipping containers laid next to each other with swings, rope walls, spin bars, and floor spikes separating them. The moving parts had a consistent whoosh, like they were running off a cycle. There was normal gymnasium equipment scattered below the course, like basketballs, weights, and padded mats.

Agent Sol slapped Bob on the back. "Well," she said, "let's get to it."

Bob followed the floor signs to the entrance of the obstacle course. The course started with a rope dangling from the ceiling, which Bob climbed easily and then used to swing to the starting platform. Agent Sol watched with her arms crossed. She was too far away for Bob to figure out her facial expression and whether he was doing this right. He shrugged and continued up to a metal grate platform. The starting platform was staged like the entrance of a car wash. Bright blue curvy letters spelled out *obstacle course*. Inside the structure, which was no wider than ten feet, were two moving columns made of hundreds of microfiber clothes. The columns quickly spun along a track that moved toward Bob, then retreated. He snickered. This was going to be a piece of cake.

He stretched his foot out to see if the microfiber would hurt. It slapped the side of his shoe and spun him until he lost his balance. Bob almost tumbled off the edge onto the gymnasium floor, but his fingers snagged the edge, and he pulled himself up. Agent Sol let out a taunt and laughed. Bob rubbed his sore foot and got back to his feet. He waited for a couple of rotations and then tried again once he learned the pattern.

The left column moved deeper into the obstacle course, and Bob lagged behind it like a shadow. Once it started turning back, he leaped to the right and sprinted so the right column couldn't clip him from behind. Bob dove to make sure he was safe and then let out a sigh of relief.

Ahead of him was a similar cyclical whirl, but this one sounded faster and sharper—like a blender. Bob scaled a climbing net to another metal platform. As he squatted to catch his breath, Bob saw that this next part was on a wider platform with no walls, allowing him to see Agent Sol watching from the side. She gave a thumbs up, clapped and whistled encouragingly.

"Let's go, newbie!" she said. "Bit of advice: Don't test this one."

Upside-down mops, about hip high, spun at ridiculous speeds. Each mop thread had a shiny, reflective tip that Bob quickly realized was a razor blade. They were moving in random directions, gliding along the floor. There wasn't even a track. He watched for half a minute, trying to spot some sort of pattern, but didn't have any luck. Each time he mapped a potential course, one mop changed its path. Bob gulped. That new mop definitely would've done some serious damage.

Bob fell back onto his butt and tapped his foot. Agent Sol called out from below.

"Don't give up! You got this, Agent Bob!"

He gave her a quick look back, followed by a thumbs up. She was watching. Oh! So were the cameras! He was on film, and this was a scene. They were rolling, and he needed to give the studio a reason to call him back for the next production. Maybe he'd get a starring role!

Think, he told himself. What would his character do? His character probably wouldn't know how to solve it immediately either. He would take time to think, do something innocuous, and then realize how to get past the challenge. Bob leaned to the side and noticed he was beneath the blades. The rods holding the spinning blade mop threads weren't ominous looking at all. They just looked like mop handles. Bob rolled onto his stomach and started crawling underneath. There was half a foot between him and the mop blades. It wasn't super comforting as the spinning gusts tickled the hairs on the back of his neck, but he made it through with no cuts.

The platform ended, and Bob leaped into a tube. He slid, feet first, into a pool of soapy water. Bubbles covered the top and reflected the ceiling lights. The area was closed off, maybe eight feet high, ten feet wide, and thirty feet long. The pool was as wide, almost as long, and shallow enough to reach the bottom for most of it. After a few seconds, he waded through the pool and pulled himself out. Straight ahead stood two glass doors covered in thick dirt. Some writing above the doorframes said *It's important to see through the pane.*

Bob licked his finger and slid it against the glass. For a second it cleared, but then the window fogged up and he couldn't see again.

He remembered calling his mom for a similar issue. It was right after he moved out and got his own place. Bob rarely helped with the cleaning, so having to do it in his studio was a bit of a learning curve. The counters were easy. He just hit them with some wipes. The dishes were simple.

He just threw them into the dishwasher. But it was the windows that defeated him. He would use water and a paper towel, but they had a weird fogginess. He tried using a bath towel, but it left streaks and tiny scratches. His mom started off with '*I told you so*' and some sarcastic quips before she revealed the secret to cleaning glass required its own solution.

Bob sniffed his sleeves that were soaked from the pool. It smelled like soap—not soapy water. He ran back and pushed aside some bubbles. Underneath was the blue liquid he realized was the only way to clean glass. He slipped off his T-shirt and gave it a quick dip in the window cleaning pool. He wrung it out and ran back to the glass doors.

He could hear his mom in his head. *Circles. Clean in circles.* He wiped vigorously, and the fog disappeared, revealing more words. The door on the left said, *Use this door*, and the one on the right said, *Wrong door*. He swung open the left door and kept going.

The area opened again except for the circular free-standing wall to his right, which had five-foot rods shaped like plungers sticking out along the edge. The wall spanned a divide between the platform Bob stood on and a similar platform on the other side. As Bob approached, there was a groan, and the wall started rotating. To his right, a small high-top table held a plastic bucket filled with white powder. Bob stared at the powder then at Agent Sol, who rubbed her temples before pointing at her hand.

"It's so you don't slip from sweat or the solution you were just swimming in," she said.

Bob felt tiny and childish for assuming it had a more intense use.

He coated his hands then leaped out and caught the first bar. The rotating wall carried him to the other side, but it was too far for him to just dismount safely. Bob swung his legs back and forth, the momentum carrying him through a swing, then another. As he approached the other ledge, he threw his weight and sailed to the final platform, landing with a tumble.

"I thought you got motion sickness," Agent Sol said.

"Only in cars and planes, things like that. Horses, too, I guess. Hadn't had that one come up before," Bob said. He continued into a closed-off section of the obstacle course.

Bob rubbed his eyes because, for a second, he thought the door teleported him to the Great Plains. There was nothing but grass for what looked to be miles, but the obstacle course couldn't be that big. He walked to the right with his hands out until he hit a wall. It was the most realistic painting, and now the room didn't seem so ridiculously large.

However, it was serene. It was quiet aside from the speakers playing bird-chirping noises. He walked back to the center of the room and took a breath. When he closed his eyes, he could hear Agent Sol's muffled voice. It sounded urgent, but he couldn't hear through the wall and over the chirps. She must have to step away or something and was just letting him know.

Hanging next to the entrance was a small handheld vacuum. It was bright red with a yellow piece of tape above it. Written on the tape in black Sharpie was *Don't forget this*. Bob picked it up cautiously then stared up at the ceiling, waiting for something to happen. Some boulder to roll through and crush him. Nothing.

Bob let out a sigh of relief and started walking slowly to the other side, over the grass. It was a straight shot to another wooden platform and bright green door on the other side. One step. The grass crunched under his feet like no one had watered it. Some dust kicked up, and he took the next step.

Crunch. The bird-chirping faded away, replaced by scurrying behind the walls.

Crunch. Bob stopped and looked around.

With a sliding whoosh, small little mouse-sized doors opened along the sides of the wall. A flash scurried out, and the door slammed shut. As he spun to spot one, it vanished, another flash shooting past his peripherals. Bob took a couple of steps back onto the platform and it all stopped. The mouse doors opened, and whatever came out bolted back in. The same thing happened when he tried crossing without the handheld vacuum, so Bob held onto it.

He started his journey once more. About halfway through, he spotted one of them—a gray, grainy-looking bunny robot. Its fur looked absolutely real as it sat still and stared at him with red dot robot eyes and a closed mouth that sent chills down Bob's spine. Bob squatted down to get a better look, and the one between him and the exit hopped to him. A second later, the other bunny robots did the same in unison.

They got closer and closer, then the mechanical whirling started up as their mouths turned into garbage disposals. Their mouths shot open, tiny razor blades lining their mouths like a tunnel and spinning around like little tornados of pain.

The first one leaped at Bob's knee. He hastily jumped out of the way and swatted the bunny with the hand vacuum. The uninjured bunny turned around to attack again. The other bunnies launched their own volleys, most narrowly missing.

Most.

Bob felt a scrape along his right arm, then a bunny

latched onto his thigh. He smacked it off, but the bunny's fangs left a circular cut. Bob's blood stained the front of the bunny's mouth, making it look even more terrifying. Bob was so distracted by the man-eating bunny in front of him that it took him an extra second to notice he accidentally clicked the handheld vacuum's power button. The handheld vacuum let out a dull drone as the engine started.

Argh! Bob cried out. A bunny lashed onto the center of his back. The razors tore through the back of his shirt and then into him. He desperately swung to knock it off. The handheld vacuum hit something, followed by a slurping sound telling him that something got sucked into the handheld vacuum. The pain was gone. The bunny was gone. Bob smirked. It was his turn.

Bob swung at another bunny. It folded onto itself and vanished into the handheld vacuum. One after another, Bob sucked them up into the handheld vacuum. Suddenly, he was on the other side. There was a piece of paper with another message. It said, *Looks like you listened.* Bob put the handheld vacuum on the docking station on this side of the room and proceeded through.

The obstacle course opened back up, and Agent Sol stood clapping on the sidelines. He was on a square wooden platform about four feet by four feet. A button next to the door read, *Push me.*

"I'm glad you read the message! I didn't think you could hear me. Those dust bunnies are vicious!" she said, her voice echoing in the massive hangar housing the obstacle course.

"So, what is all this for?" he said. Bob looked down at his cuts and bruises from the bunnies. Veritably didn't say Bob had to do his own stunts, but Bob would do anything to get into Veritably's good graces and get cast in future shows...or maybe even a movie. Bob just wanted a little heads up to prepare for blunt weapons, sharp weapons, and killer robot bunnies.

"Practice. Being one of us, you never know what can come up. Gotta be ready for anything. Use your head," Agent Sol said.

"Us being…"

"Agents."

Great. They were still filming.

Bob nodded. He threw his head back, took a breath, and jogged in place. Ahead of him was a thin plank, twenty feet long and a mere five inches wide, leading to the other side. Underneath and perpendicular to it was a long metal pipe as wide as the platform holding Bob. On the other side, a chain-link metal gate blocked the finish. Right past the gate was a large red button on top of a wooden pedestal. The word *Finish* wrapped around the base of the pedestal in bold, white lettering.

"You got this!" Agent Sol said.

Bob pressed the button, and the door swung open. He tapped a foot on the beam. It was solid. Another step. The plank stood firm. Bob was halfway through when he got close to the metal pipe. Penny-sized holes about two inches apart lined the top of the pipe. Bob waved his hand through the air in front of him, hoping to trigger whatever trap was in store. The pipe didn't react, and the gate didn't close. He glanced at Agent Sol, who just stood watching him. He gulped.

One step. Then another. Once over the pipe, he stared down into the holes, waiting for the surprise to catch him. Each one looked like an endless void holding an impossible number of cleaning-related obstacles. Bob imagined some disturbing shimmer and hyper-focused on each hole he could see. No need to wait and see if he was hallucinating or some unimaginable danger was going to erupt from the pipe. Bob made a beeline across the plank and dove onto the final platform. He crawled to the pedestal and slammed the button.

Confetti rained from the ceiling above him, and trumpets blared from the speakers in the platforms and ceiling. They drowned out Agent Sol's clapping, but Bob saw her doing it. He returned a thumbs up and turned on the smile he practiced in the mirror for his headshots. Judging from how her face reacted, he needed to practice more. He made a goofy face and hoped he could play it off as a joke.

Once the celebrations and trumpets stopped, Bob took a slide down to the ground floor and chuckled.

"Good job, Bob. You earned yourself a nice break," Agent Sol said.

Bob let out a sigh of relief. It was nice to get a break from filming. At least it sounded like they stopped.

"So, how did I do?" he said.

Agent Sol had a wide smile on her face.

"Way better than I thought you'd do."

"Better than that Agent Lorox guy?"

She frowned and headed out the door. "Come on. We should report back."

Chapter Five

They went back to the briefing room. Bob made sure to jog ahead and enter the code Agent Sol taught him. Even better, the thumbprint scanner had a note over it: *Temporarily disabled.* He mumbled to himself.

"48...23...1787. Hygienic."

The door unlocked, and he held it open for Agent Sol to walk through. Her face was still stone, the same as it was the entire way back to the briefing room, and Bob's stomach grew heavy. He wanted to apologize again, but he didn't want to annoy her. He'd just have to show that he was sorry.

Before he could pull out a chair for her, Agent Sol took her own seat and texted something on her phone, then slipped it back into her pocket. Bob took a seat a few away from her on the other side of the table. He said, "So what's the plan?"

"The plan is to wait here. Director Veritably wants to congratulate you personally and get you fitted for the next assignment. You're going into the field."

That had to be slang for getting an important role.

Bob's hairline and palms started sweating. It was everything he'd worked for. He imagined the red-carpet walks! The endorsements! The magazine articles saying *Bob Johnson is just like you.* His parents would be so proud. Maybe they could even get into that club they wanted. He smiled. Maybe there would be articles about how he met his current girlfriend and former co-star. He looked over to her then stifled his smile to match Agent Sol's mood.

"Is that the real deal? This was all an audition?" he said.

"Audition? What? Like a tryout? Yeah, sort of. You're a part of the agency already, but we wanted to see what skill level you had. If we gave you too big a role, it would jeopardize everything we do here."

Bob's heart raced. He didn't have any on-camera speaking experience. What if they pushed him into a role he wasn't ready for? Bob needed time with a script to learn his lines or get a feel for the character. Was he just supposed to learn it on the fly? That's so different from what his teachers and coaches taught him. That's like a decades-in-the-industry ability, and he hadn't done this for very long.

"Don't get nervous," Agent Sol said. "That obstacle course is tough, and you ran through it in record time."

Bob let out a nervous chuckle. "Yeah, I know. I just don't want to mess up, you know? There is just a lot of pressure, and my coaches, they invested a lot of time in me, and my parents—"

"Bob, you're rambling again," she said with a playful chuckle. Bob just nodded quickly then put his hands in his lap.

"So, now what?"

"We wait. Director is running a little late."

"Is something wrong?"

"Nah, he's probably just busy. Nothing bad ever happens here."

Boom! The room shook, releasing a thin layer of dust to the ground below. Agent Sol shot to her feet, drawing a gun from the holster at her side. Her face looked concerned and laser-focused. Bob was really impressed. That must've been the cue to start the scene. It was unorthodox, but it really sold the idea that danger lurked around the corner.

"Agent Sol, status update," Bob said, standing up so quickly that the chair shot backward and slammed into the wall. He cringed. The studio might take the set damage out of his paycheck.

"Sit rep unknown, Agent Bob. Potential unplanned engagement at our current location," she said. Agent Sol scanned him then said, "Where's your gun?"

"I was never issued one, Agent Sol," Bob said with a smoldering look. He spotted a nearby security camera stuck in a ceiling corner. He adjusted his position so it could get a good shot of his face, but he didn't look at it. "I'll just have to pry one from the cold hands of anyone who tries me."

"Right...I'll take point."

Agent Sol kicked open the door and Bob followed. He ran lines in his head, trying to come up with a witty response, but decided that Agent Sol had more experience, so she should get the last line of a scene. He was okay with being a supporting character. That's how all the greats start. He'd get his time. After crushing that obstacle course and that awesome line before, he'd definitely get more spots.

Alarms blared. Red and white lights spun around, bathing the set in an ominous glow. Black suit actors, weapons drawn, sprinted down the hall past them toward the vehicle hangar. They didn't pay Bob or Agent Sol any mind. Agent Sol grabbed one of them by the arm and said, "What's going on?"

The black suit actress whipped off her sunglasses and held them at her side. She squinted and said, "They're here. D.I.R.T. is attacking and they've taken the director." The black suit actress slid her sunglasses back on and continued toward the hangar.

Bob smiled. Professionals were amazing. The line delivery, the cadence, and the prop usage were all amazing. He didn't have any comments. Suddenly, Agent Sol punched him in the chest.

"Why are you smiling? This is serious! Let's go!" she said.

Bob squeezed his hand. He stupidly broke character and was grateful that Agent Sol called him out. She even did so in character. Bob had a lot to learn from her.

The two followed the crowd until they reached a four-way intersection. To the right was the TV monitor wall room. To the left was the hangar, and straight ahead was another hallway that kept summoning agents.

"Take cover!" someone said. Bob knew how scenes like this went down. It was time for the supporting character to save the main hero at the cost of his own life. He yanked Agent Sol back and covered her with his body.

Boom! Bob's ears rang, and then he felt something burn his back. It seared through his own suit and slid down like oozing magma. The burning pain forced him to a knee. Agent Sol was saying something as she squatted next to him. He couldn't hear it over the ringing. She felt his forehead. Her hand was ice cold. She pulled off his jacket. The heat vanished, but the burn was still there. Bob fell back against the wall and took heavy breaths.

Dozens of injured black suit actors rolled on the floor as

the uninjured ones tended to them. Agent Dawn dragged two black suit actors behind cover all while yelling something. Agents rushed past her like tidal waves to provide cover.

The ringing in Bob's ears slowly faded away. Agent Sol worriedly stared into his eyes.

"Thank God you're back. Are you okay?"

Bob nodded. His back wasn't hurting as much, but he could still feel the concentrated pain like a really nasty sunburn. He forced himself to his feet, and Agent Sol swooped under his shoulders and helped him up.

"There you go," she said.

The ceiling lights flickered, and red splotches covered the walls. People cried out, likely from the same pain Bob felt. One black suit actor was on his knees, holding his red-stained button-down shirt in his arms like an injured friend. Were they acting, or were they really hurt like Bob?

"Get the stain removers! We need soaking water, ASAP," Agent Dawn said, her voice booming over the gunfire.

Projectiles flew in both directions, into the facility and out into the hangar. The ones that missed the C.L.E.A.N. agents splattered against the sheetrock inside the facility, leaving a small indent and a light red stain.

Bob took his jacket from the floor and smelled the back. It was marinara sauce. His eyes went wide. This sauce was a nightmare to get out of clothes, especially white button-downs that were a standard part of the C.L.E.A.N. uniform.

He suddenly understood everyone's frustration. These C.L.E.A.N. "agents" prided themselves on being clean so much, it was their entire identity. A stain or spill on their uniforms was no less painful than being shot or burned.

Then, D.I.R.T. came around unprovoked and sullied them. Bob remembered all the times he had a white-collared shirt or dress shirt that fit just right, but he had to throw it away because of the infamous Italian sauce. They went too far. These D.I.R.T. actors provided great motivation. He finally clicked with the character in this show. Bob snorted like an enraged bull, ready to stampede.

Agent Sol must've seen the look in his eyes because she grabbed a gun from a grieving agent and tossed it to Bob.

"It's time we clean up this mess," she said. Bob gave a slow and confident nod.

"I just can't stain-d these guys," he said. He popped out the magazine, a skill he picked up in acting class. Inside were pellet-sized red and blue projectiles that looked like laundry gel pods. Producers must use this for tracking and make it look like bullets in post-production. He clicked the magazine back in and took off the safety. The prop gun in his hand was a lot heavier than the props he was used to working with. But this was the real deal. Heavy equipment was an industry trick to make muscles bulge more. He would give whoever was in charge exactly what they wanted.

Bob unbuttoned his shirt and tossed it off, leaving only his sleeveless undershirt to cover his torso. A black suit actor passed, pushing a cart covered with cases of water bottles. Bob snatched one and poured it over himself so he looked sweaty, his white undershirt squeezing against his muscles.

Agent Sol's jaw dropped and her cheeks blushed, and once they made eye contact, she got back into character.

"Yeah, um, I guess that was a good use of the water. Let's just try to keep it for the downed agents, okay?"

Bob made his way to the edge of the wall. He peered into the hangar and spotted the enemy. There were five right by the hangar entrance peeking their heads into the doorway, shooting, then ducking back into cover. One of their shots hit a black suit actress, who collapsed screaming. Bob rushed over and inspected where she was hit. He removed her hand that clasped the injury and recognized it as a red wine stain. These D.I.R.T. actors were ruthless.

They wore white suits, covered in dirt, grime, and oil. The suits were so dirty that it was a stretch to call them white—more like a dingy yellow. Their hair was disheveled, and they wore strapped sandals that highlighted their gross, ungroomed feet. One toenail was at least three inches long!

Agent Sol moved to the injured black suit actress. She had taken a bottle of water and was dabbing at one of the marinara stains.

"How do we beat them?" he said.

"We need to focus on preservation. We don't have the numbers for a rescue op."

"Rescue op? Who was captured?"

"Director Veritably."

Bob knew his character wouldn't leave Director Veritably in the hands of these monsters.

"Incoming!" someone shouted. A bright red tomato sailed through the air into the intersection.

"Grenade!" another person said.

They were right. At another look, the red color came from the marinara held inside a plastic shell, the grenade top painted green to mirror a tomato stem. It landed right next to Agent Dawn, who was protecting other agents and couldn't evade in time. Bob sprinted at the grenade and tossed it back into the hangar. The heat from the grenade seared his hand. After finishing his throw, Bob rolled back into cover on Agent Dawn's side of the intersection. They acknowledged each other, and she continued organizing the remaining black suit actors.

The D.I.R.T. actors, terrified from the grenade, retreated from the door. Bob charged forward. He spotted a couple of D.I.R.T. actors fleeing and fired gel pellets, each exploding against their backs and lifting the stains from their dirty suits. Also, from the sound the pellet made when it hit their backs, it hurt...a lot. The enemies fell to the ground upon impact and crawled into cover, shouting back, "Ow! How dare you!"

Injury for D.I.R.T. actors must work the same way it does for C.L.E.A.N. agents. One of the D.I.R.T. actors Bob shot grabbed some dirt from the floor and rubbed it on the suit, though he winced in pain as he did it.

Bob waved at his fellow actors to advance. He slipped into the hangar and dove behind some crates and barrels. The buses, tanks, and planes were crudely shoved against the walls, so they toppled over each other like a disorganized child's toy box. The cleared hangar had crates scattered every few feet, tire towers about six feet high scattered about, and pallets of laundry detergent closer to where Bob stood. The D.I.R.T. actors must've set them up between scenes to use as cover.

At the other end of the hangar, the opened doors looked out over a desert. But what grabbed Bob's attention the most was the massive block-looking thing covered by a dingy green and crusty blanket.

Agent Sol slid right next to Bob with a ferocity in her eyes. Bob stifled a smile. This show was going to be awesome, but they had to pull off this scene.

Agent Sol tapped on the barrel with her gun. "If you kick this out, I can explode it and we can push these guys back," she said. Bob peeked over the crates, and a stream of red wine flew past his face. It was so close he could smell the earthy, bitter aromas of a traditional red wine, yet when it crashed into the cement wall it left a small crater. Bob ducked back to cover. He reminded himself that it was all just special effects, and he wasn't actually in danger. That didn't mean a small part of him wasn't still worried.

"They deployed the wine snipers. Let's go," Agent Sol said.

He tipped the barrel over on its side, then pushed it down one of the marked aisles where it rolled toward a pocket of D.I.R.T. actors. A couple glanced at it, but they just laughed.

"You missed!" one D.I.R.T. actor said. Agent Sol pulled a magazine out of her back pocket and swapped it with the one in her prop gun. She rolled out from behind the crates and fired.

The barrel exploded, launching blue liquid in every direction. The D.I.R.T. actors cried out as the drops crashed into them, sizzling on their skin.

"Stop cleaning us!"

Bob dashed ahead to a tire tower. Agent Sol carefully advanced to a crate. The other actors provided cover fire. Even they looked like amazing actors. Whenever one took a hit from a wine blast or marinara grenade, they really acted like it hurt. The wounds and burns looked so realistic.

Beeping rang out—the kind a truck made when backing up. Two dump trucks unloaded tons of dirt behind the covered object. Once their beds were empty, they retreated to the desert.

Two D.I.R.T. actors sprinted to the large, covered box. Bob fired and narrowly missed. The D.I.R.T. actors yanked off the green blanket, revealing a wall of industrial-sized fans ten feet tall and thirty feet wide.

"Retreat!" Agent Sol said, running back. "Bob! What are you waiting for? You won't survive this."

Bob nodded. That had to be his cue to be a hero. He knew somewhere Director Veritably, or whoever was in charge, was watching.

The fans hummed, then spun. The gust was so strong, the tire tower Bob stood behind wobbled. It was an interesting prop, but Bob couldn't figure out why people were running. Agent Sol sure looked terrified, though.

"Launch!" one of the D.I.R.T. actors said. They shoveled some dirt and tossed it into the fan, launching it like bullets. Like a spear, one pebble ripped through the tires hiding Bob. These fans were suddenly much more dangerous than the previous stunts. Agent Sol had made it past the blue door into the main building and behind the cover, but other actors were caught in the blast. Some dropped to the floor, their jacket backs studded with pebbles. Bob hoped they had some sort of padding because it really looked painful.

There was a lull, and Bob dashed over to the crates where he started.

"Launch!"

The pebble volley decimated the tire tower. Rubber shrapnel sprayed in hundreds of directions and settled on the unconscious C.L.E.A.N. agents on the floor. His character would probably save them, but Bob didn't get a cue or see how he could. Plus, they seemed safe where they were. The pebbles swept right over them without hitting them. They might just get dusty. No one was in real danger.

Agent Sol leaned out and waved Bob to hurry. He nodded and sprinted toward her.

"Launch!"

Adrenaline kicked in. Bob actually felt the danger. This

was a really good acting experience. The invisible director timed the lines perfectly, and the supporting enemy actors did great. Everything slowed down. He heard his heart beating, then the gargle of the rocks, dirt, and pebbles swirling around the fan. They all whistled as the projectiles launched in his direction. Little puffs crashed into the wall or smashed through the crates Bob used for cover. Splinters rained down and snagged themselves in his clothing and hair. He wanted to look back and see the effects, but he couldn't blow the scene. If they could do this in one take, that would be amazing. He couldn't ruin it. Bob would just have to watch it in—

Sphhhlt! He felt a sharp pain in his thigh. His leg gave out, and he violently crashed a foot away from the door, his face scraping against the cement floor. Agent Sol reached out and dragged him into cover and another black suit actor slammed the door behind them a second before what sounded like gunshots pelted the door.

Bob screamed. It hurt more than he could describe. The center of the pain was his right thigh, but it radiated throughout his leg. He squirmed and thrashed like lightning was trapped under his skin. Nothing alleviated the feeling.

"Dammit! Shit!" he cried out.

Bob looked down at his wound. He was bleeding. Badly. He signed up for a comedy—not this bullshit. The risk must be why the greats used stunt doubles. He didn't know if this was part of the script or an accident. It must be part of the script because no one yelled cut. Bob wanted to get angry and yell, but he didn't want to ruin anything more and have to refilm this. So, he sat in angry silence since it hurt too much to think about anything else.

"Bob! Stay with me, okay?" Agent Sol said. She positioned him so he could sit up against the wall. Then she looked up. "Medic!" Someone rushed over and cut away his right pant leg.

This was too real. Bob lurched forward as vomit surged up his throat, but he held it back. He couldn't look at his leg. The glimpse he'd had was enough to send him spiraling. He stared at the marinara- and wine-covered ceiling now the color of blood. He was bleeding. Worse now. Bob felt queasy again.

"Hey, Bob, look at me," Agent Sol said. She grabbed Bob by the chin and smiled.

"Just look at me, Bob. Things are okay. You're gonna be fine. This is a totally normal thing, and we're going to fix it, okay?" Bob stared into her eyes, which were slightly calming. He didn't want to speak, so he just nodded to show he was listening.

"You're doing great, okay?" she said. "Agent Tastic is going to take care of your leg."

Bob twitched at the mention of his leg.

"Okay, I'll tell you about things. So..." Agent Sol's voice faded away as Bob's eyes wandered to all the people running back and forth. Cracked lights sneezed out sparks. Blasts of wine and marinara grenades ruined the walls, knocked down the posters, and shattered most of the screens in the monitor room way past Bob.

One showed a video of Director Veritably bound and fighting to get free. He was in the back of some truck. Sitting next to him was someone who looked familiar. Someone who looked like Charlie.

"Back here, Bob," Agent Sol said, tapping him on the cheek. "So, I really like donuts. Getting donuts is my favorite thing to do." Then she listed off an endless variety of donuts, almost all of which Bob never heard of. It might've been whatever Agent Tastic injected him with or the blood loss making him go loopy, but it kind of sounded like Agent Sol started naming donuts in other languages. Bob let his head clunk against the wall. Would he have to learn other languages to be an actor?

A cold sensation suddenly started around his elbow. It swam up and down his arm and through the rest of his body. His heart slowed, and he felt calm. His eyelids got heavy, and Bob instinctually hit snooze.

* * *

"Don't worry, Agent Sol. He's stable," Agent Tastic said, continuing to care for Bob after he fell asleep. He pulled out more gauze and medicine from his bag.

Agent Lila Sol nodded and thanked Agent Tastic again. She knew he wasn't ready. This was Bob's first day on the job, and she threw him into high-stakes combat. Even if he excelled at the physical challenges, combat takes mental fortitude. He had probably only seen combat in movies. At least that was how he was acting—like this was just a movie.

She looked back at him with a raised eyebrow, remembering how he talked and the words he used and the fact that he was an extra when she met him on set. Was he—

"All able agents, circle up!" Agent Dawn said, her voice the only thing louder than the barrage of rocks and pebbles battering the concrete hangar wall. Every agent looked up to her in awe. "Things do not look great. Many of us are injured. Some of us are in the clutches of those D.I.R.T. scumbags. But...today showed us that there are heroes in all of us. Agent Bob has been with us for just one day and has served as an inspiration. He set an agency record on the 'Newbie Killer', invented a technique to reduce the effectiveness of D.I.R.T. weapons, and led the pushback on the enemy. Now, I personally refuse to let some childish assholes come into my house and make my home dirty. I'm going out there and kicking them out. You can stay here and be fine. But if you do, many years from now, you'll look back and wonder what if. What if you had stood beside me, beside Director Veritably, beside Agent Bob? What if you took this one chance to tell our enemies that they may stain our clothes and hurt our bodies, but they'll never take our cleanliness!"

The crowd erupted around her like dozens of volcanoes. Their screams were louder than the enemy on the other side of the wall.

Agent Sol looked at Bob one more time. She'd figure him out when they were safe. For now, she'd carry on his example. After lifting whatever ammo and weapons he had in his pockets, she stood up and prepared for combat.

Agents poured out from every crevasse of C.L.E.A.N. headquarters. About ten were covered in standard C.L.E.A.N. body gear, which was stronger than Kevlar and looked like it was built from mop buckets, sponges and dust-pans. Other agents came in with heavy weapons, including the M47 CLEAN, a detergent blaster that resembled a giant plunger, or the Mini-Bottle, a heavy machine gun with a large showerhead that shot all-purpose cleaning solutions at lethal speeds.

Once the injured agents, including Bob, were evacuated to the medical wing, Agent Dawn stood at the front of her squadron of agents. "On my mark." The body-armor agents moved to the front.

The barrage continued against the wall. A long time passed as they equipped their agents. Without interference, the D.I.R.T. agents attacked without restraint. Unfortunately, they made a lot of progress. The impact of dirt and pebbles crashing into the hangar wall had grown louder than when they first closed the door, likely from them chipping away pieces of the cement wall. Without a doubt, if they did nothing, C.L.E.A.N. would soon fall. The world would be plunged into an unsanitary and unregulated nightmare.

"Hold!" Agent Dawn raised a fist.

Agent Sol bit her lip and waited, right behind the body armor agents. The barrage continued. Little pockets of light shone through the wall, just barely large enough for debris to get through.

"Hold!"

Agent Sol thought of all her training. All the agents she met that were lost defending this country and the world from terrorist organizations. All the ways she thought she was going to die. She never imagined this. Making one last stand on their home turf.

"Go!"

The body-armor agents kicked open the hangar door and activated their shields, which were mop heads spinning at the speed of sound and strands formed from titanium. The D.I.R.T. projectiles and weapons bounced off and fell harmlessly to the ground. Agent Sol followed them, remembering her training from the Newbie Killer obstacle course. She kept her hand on the shoulder of the agent right in front of her.

"Fire!" a D.I.R.T. agent said, signaling another barrage.

"As you were trained! Don't you dare back down!" Agent Dawn burst through the door and sprinted to cover behind a totaled fighter jet. "Down!"

Agent Sol dove to the ground as a swarm of rocks sailed over her and destroyed anything unlucky enough to get in its way. She looked forward and saw a couple of the body-armor agents fall.

"Third line, evac!" Agent Dawn said.

The agents behind Agent Sol sprinted forward and dragged the injured agents to cover, or if necessary, treated them there.

"Fourth line, go!"

All of the vents in the hangar ceiling burst open and a dozen C.L.E.A.N. agents rained down, firing at the enemy as they descended. The enemy fired back, sometimes severing the rappel in the process.

"Sol! Eyes up!"

Agent Sol nodded and caught up to her assigned body-armor agent, peeking out to fire with pinpoint accuracy at the D.I.R.T. agents who attacked her partner. They advanced.

Boom! The sound of the M47 Clean. A wave of hygiene impact pellets, slightly larger than the ones in Agent Sol's weapon, exploded past them like a pack of vicious wolves, ripping into and taking down their targets. Then, C.L.E.A.N. agents fired the Mini-Bottle, which reverberated like hundreds of popping carbonated bottles, launching jet streams of a light green liquid past them and exploding the D.I.R.T. agents' cover. The wine snipers fired in retaliation, taking out some of the C.L.E.A.N. artillery.

"Go! Go! Don't you dare stop!"

Agent Sol signaled her partner that she was breaking off and sprinted to the fan. The bullets whooshed past her in both directions, but she didn't flinch, even as they whistled past her ear or tore through the loose fabric of her clothing.

The fan was close. A D.I.R.T. agent tried to intercept her, but she slid, took out his feet, then chopped his throat as he fell to the ground. Another fired at her, but she narrowly dodged his slugs. She flung two clothes pins from her belt at the agent's face. He deflected them, but they bought her enough time to tackle him to the floor. She snatched the gun from his hand and slammed his head against the floor, knocking him out cold. Another D.I.R.T. agent charged at her, but she whipped the emptied enemy gun at him, knocking him to the ground.

The D.I.R.T. agents operating the fan fled, leaving Agent Sol alone with the horrific contraption. She began to sigh in relief but then realized that before they fled, they had prepared one last volley. With dozens of her fellow agents in the line of fire, Agent Sol darted to the controls, desperately trying to find some way to stop the machine.

Unfortunately, the control panel was busted. She kicked the machine in frustration, and her foot snagged on something. A wire! Lila pulled out her pistol and fired at the wire plugged into the machine. There was a burst of sparks and the machine shut down.

Agent Sol collapsed to the floor, staring up at the ceiling. It was a really long day.

Chapter Six

It was the heart monitor's rhythmic beeping that gently woke up Bob. He took his customary nostril inhale, which was stuffier than normal, and subconsciously stretched out like he was going to hit snooze on his alarm clock.

"Bob!" Agent Sol said, sitting in a chair beside him. She snatched his wrists before he moved too much. "You gotta go slow, okay?" She undid a strip of tape under his nose and gently pulled out long clear tubes. Air rushed in as Bob sniffed.

He was in a small white room just large enough for his bed and about four feet on each side, with heavy white blankets and sheets wrapped so tightly around him he could barely move his legs. The head of the bed was raised, so he sat up with his head resting on a comfy pillow.

Things were a little fuzzy. Then he remembered what had happened before he woke up. His leg throbbed. Bob glanced around. There were no cameras in this room. It was just him and Agent Sol, though she looked a little more beat up than when he saw her last. He took a deep breath. They looked in between scenes, and he had a lot to get off his chest. Either way, he didn't care at this point if he ruined the scene. Things had gone too far. He got burned and basically shot in the leg. There was no script. There was no one directing. There was no feedback. Bob was tired of guessing what his character would do. It was a fun challenge at first, but this was chaotic. Bob wanted order—not an ad-libbed production. This wasn't professional. It felt like a ten-year-old trust-fund kid ran the show, and Bob was tired of it. No station or streaming service in its right mind would pay for this.

"Why am I in a hospital bed?" Bob said.

"The pebble that hit your thigh got lodged in there, so they had to put you under to take it out. It was a minor—"

"Don't tell me 'surgery.' Please don't tell me you guys put me under without even asking me," Bob said. His heart pounded against his chest, and he started trembling. "What kind of series is this, huh? You, you, you don't even wake me up for the briefing. I get to the briefing, but no one tells me when we start filming. And this plot. My God, how is anyone supposed to believe this thing? Really? *Washing machine* security? You think *anyone* is going to get the idea that the government is funding this nonsense? You guys sure as hell spent enough money on the set. I hope you got enough to cover the cost of this surgery." Bob let out a quick exhale and collapsed onto his pillow. "I'm sorry. I had to get that off my chest." He flicked his hand around. "We can restart the scene or whatever. Or fire me. I don't really care at this point. You guys aren't professional at all. I've done high school plays with better production. I'll happily take my check and leave."

Agent Sol pursed her lips and stared intently at Bob like she was slowly processing his rant. His anger vanished under her gaze. She wasn't in charge of this thing, but he snapped at her. He was a total jerk.

"I'm sorry. I shouldn't flip out on you. It's just I woke up, and I don't like surgery, and you were the first person I saw. I don't even know who's in charge of this thing. I thought it was that Veritably guy, but then I saw he was in the scene getting captured. Is he one of those directors that puts himself in his own movie or like—I'm rambling again. I'm sorry."

Agent Sol shook her head and leaned back. Then she chewed on her lower lip and ran her hand through her hair.

"Bob, where do you think you are?"

"In some hospital or something. I don't know."

"What do you think my profession is?"

Bob squinted. "Are we filming?"

"No, Bob, we aren't filming. This is just two people talking to each other. No pretending."

"You're an actress, right? Or maybe you got like another part-time job or something."

"Something like that." She placed her hand by her temple. "And D.I.R.T. You think they're fake, right?"

"Yeah, Dastardly...something, something team? Sorry, I never got a script."

"Never got a script..." Agent Sol leaned back in her chair, stared up at the ceiling, and chuckled.

"What's so funny?"

Agent Sol paced around the room as she dialed some number on her cell phone.

"What's so funny! You know what? This is real mature, okay."

Whoever she called sent her to voicemail. She hung up with a disappointed look on her face and plopped into her chair.

"Bob," she said, "you're really not going to like what I have to say."

The door slammed open, the knob lodging itself into the wall, and Agent Dawn stormed into the room. She'd changed from her dress into a blue Kevlar-looking outfit. Her hair was tied back into a bun, and blue glasses covered her eyes. She wore a blue vest with at least ten different pockets, which covered a tight polyester long-sleeve shirt. Her pants, also blue, had another twenty pockets and were tucked into pristine white combat boots. Agent Dawn's presence was so commanding that she hid the short black suit actor standing behind her.

"Agent Bob," she said, "good to see you're awake."

Bob raised his hands in surrender and shook his head. "Dawn, I'm sorry. I only know you as Dawn. I was just telling Agent Sol here that I—"

"There's no time for this. Agents Sol and Bob, you are the only ones I can trust to rescue Director Veritably."

"No! I've had enough of—"

Agent Sol leapt from her seat and yelled, "Action!"

A switch flicked in Bob's head. Finally, he had direction. Finally, he could separate reality from a scene. Finally, he could act. He cleared his throat and activated his smoldering face.

Chapter Seven

"What's the mission, Director?" Bob said. He made his voice gravelly but bold—exactly what a spy should sound like. Bob's coaches told him to project his voice past his co-star, so the voice carried farther and with more gravitas. It worked. His voice slammed against Agent Dawn, and it took her a second to snap back into the scene.

"Good to see you're both on board. I knew I could count on you," she said, snapping her fingers. "Agent Uloso, please shut the door."

The tan person with dark hair and goatee behind her yanked out the doorknob from the wall and gingerly closed it. Director Dawn continued.

"Agent Lorox lead the attack himself and captured Director Veritably. We've interrogated a captured D.I.R.T. agent. What we learned is that they plan to torture Veritably to get his override codes, then deactivate C.L.E.A.N. software so they can install their own. The situation could *not* be more serious."

"Permission to speak," Agent Sol said.

Director Dawn nodded.

"I'm concerned with Agent Bob's qualifications to participate in this offensive."

"Your concerns have been noted. Unfortunately, our most senior agents are either downed or on another assignment. D.I.R.T. disrupted our external communications, so we can't even relay our situation to the lesser agencies. However, Agent Bob has set a record on the obstacle course and proved his ability during the siege. Without his bravery, we would have lost more agents and wouldn't have been able to repel D.I.R.T. Agent Bob, do you accept this mission?"

Bob nodded. Agent Sol stared at him with such intensity that it looked like she was trying to tell him something telepathically. Bob noticed a vein throbbing next to her temples. He knew the message. *Act harder.*

"I'll do it if my country needs me."

"Director," Agent Sol said, "permission to carry out the engagement solo?"

"Denied. I also had my doubts, but Agent Bob has impressed me. Thanks to Bob's pre-soak technique we were able to prevent the marinara from harming our agents. He is an inspiration and single-handedly the reason why we were able to repel D.I.R.T.," she said. It took Bob a couple seconds to realize it was when he poured the water on himself.

"He even impressed Director Veritably himself," Agent Dawn said, pulling out a note from a vest pocket and handing it to Agent Sol, who read it out loud.

"'Agent Bob Johnson is immediately granted level nine clearance and should be equipped with level green equipment.' That's higher than mine," she said. Agent Sol looked dumbfounded as she handed the note back to Agent Dawn.

"Like I said, Agent Bob is a once-in-a-lifetime agent."

Bob looked back and forth between Agent Dawn and Agent Sol. He wasn't sure what was going on, so he'd just have to improvise based on their context clues. Whatever they were talking about, it sounded important. It also sounded like Bob was the main character all along.

Bob undid his blanket bindings and slid off the bed. He was a little woozy, but it quickly passed, and he stood tall.

"I can be good to move in five," he said.

Agent Dawn smiled and responded with her own smolder.

"Make it four, dammit. We'll brief you once we hit altitude." Agent Dawn spun on her heel and walked out of the room with Agent Uloso dragging behind her.

Agent Sol quickly slammed the door shut.

"Bob, I don't think you should do this."

"I have to do it! My country needs me."

"Ugh! We aren't acting. Cut."

Bob dropped his smolder and sat back on the bed. "Yeah, I mean, I wasn't crazy about it either, but I think this could be really good for me. I've never gotten an acting role. I've only been an extra, but this...this might be my break."

"Bob, this isn't a movie!"

"I know. It's a show or a series. I'm still not sure on the length."

"You're not listening!" Her voice was worried.

"I know what I said, and I know you don't think I can do this, but someone out there thinks I can. I just need you to believe in me, too. If I don't go through with this, everything we filmed before is wasted. All the other actors and stunt people acted their butts off to pull off the pain look. They're all counting on me. It wasn't like I wanted to be the main character. I literally came here as an extra. Freaking weird and pervy Linda stole my sweater, and I'm scared to think of what she's doing with it. Then I got on a bus, and here I am. If I bail, or I quit, or if my co-star doesn't believe in me, then it was all for nothing."

Agent Sol's eyes scanned Bob's face. She took a deep breath and said, "You really are something, huh? If I told you that we do all of our own stunts from here on out, you still in?"

"Yeah."

"There's no tapping out if you go into this next...scene."

"I can handle it."

"We're going to be doing dangerous things. You might take another pebble to the leg—or worse."

That made Bob pause. He looked down at his leg. He didn't realize it before, but he was wearing a hospital gown that reached down to his knees. Judging from the feeling of his butt on the mattress, he knew he wasn't wearing underwear. So instead of hiking up the skirt, he just slid his hand to where he thought the wound was. It still kind of hurt, but he remembered the scene from *Lord of the Rings* where Viggo Mortensen kicked the helmet, broke his toe, and didn't quit. Halle Berry didn't quit. Leonardo DiCaprio didn't quit. The greats got hurt in their craft and played it off. This was Bob's moment. Someday another budding actor or actress was going to watch this show or series and say, *Wow. Bob Johnson really got hurt in this scene but pushed on.*

He turned to Agent Sol, who waited patiently with a flat look on her face. Bob got to his feet, walked over, and reached out a hand. "Just let me know my motivation and my cues, and we got this." They did a power clasp where both of them grabbed the other by the forearm. After one shake, they let go. Bob then raised a finger and said, "Also, if there is any motion sickness medicine around, I'd really appreciate some."

Chapter Eight

Mrs. Johnson sighed as she carried her clothes hamper to the laundry room. Passing the living room, she gave a quick smile to her adorable husband, who was sleeping in front of the TV again. He was sprawled out as he always was in his retirement. Before she left, Mrs. Johnson raised an eyebrow at what was on the TV.

"Total Remix Interior Decoration?" she said quietly to herself. Her husband, Greg, never watched stuff like that. It was an entire channel of cheap furniture that broke or stained way too easily. Some of her friends bought from it, but they always had complaints. She rested the hamper on the five-seat couch catty-corner to Mr. Johnson's recliner. Mrs. Johnson clicked the remote, and the TV let out its usual fizz, like a balloon losing air until the screen went black. After she laid a blanket over Mr. Johnson, an electronic whine came from the kitchen.

The dishwasher was acting up again. Mr. Johnson must've forgotten to start it. With an aggravated lift of the hamper, she made her way to the kitchen. They were having company over later today and needed everything cleaned. He wasn't going to handwash everything, and she sure as heck wasn't going to either.

She did all her kitchen chores: Refilled the hand soaps, rearranged the glasses so they formed a gradient in case their guests peeked inside the cabinet, swapped out the hand towels for the "company" towels, polished the sink and stove, mopped, and waxed the floors. Greg had one job, and he didn't even do that.

"Greg," she said in her passive-aggressive tone.

"Yes, my magical queen?" Greg said back in his condescending voice.

"You didn't make sure the dishwasher was running?"

"I did, sugar plum. I remember because I had just finished hand-polishing every cabinet knob in a clockwise fashion like you asked me."

She started the dishwasher and closed it with a grunt. Mrs. Johnson stormed back to the living room and put her hands on her hips.

"You know," she said, "you could really learn to appreciate everything I do to make this house presentable."

Mr. Johnson didn't sit up in his recliner or turn to look at his wife. "Well, honey, *you* could learn that we are giving these people—most you don't even like—an unlimited bar tab and a three-course meal with a cocktail hour in our backyard for the Gomez dog's birthday." She couldn't see, but Mrs. Johnson knew her husband well enough to know when he rolled his eyes. "It's a dog's birthday. Let's remember that."

"Well, I want to get into the yacht club this year, and these people are the way in. Rumor has it that the Gomez's are going to move away soon, and we *need* their recommendation."

"Honey, we don't even have a boat. Unless Bob nails that part and becomes a movie star, we aren't going to have one large enough to satisfy their egos."

Before Mrs. Johnson could serve her own response, the dishwasher blared again.

"Umph. I'll take care of it," Mr. Johnson said, his voice depleted. The recliner's engine slowly lifted Mr. Johnson's large body, and then he groaned as he stood up and turned the TV back on. The recliner's leather let out a gasp as the cushions sucked in all the air his weight pushed out. "Also, why did you turn off my show? I was watching that."

Mrs. Johnson looked him up and down.

"You were watching TRID?"

"No, I was watching...I wasn't watching this."

Both of them turned to the kitchen and realized the dishwasher had stopped blaring and started running. Mr. Johnson shrugged his shoulders and changed the channel. Right as the Central City Goliaths scored a touchdown, the dishwasher blared again. When Mr. Johnson turned it back to the TRID channel, it stopped blaring.

"Honey, I swear I didn't do anything to the TV or the dishwasher," he said, all the sarcasm drained from his voice.

Mrs. Johnson rested a hand on his arm, gave a loving squeeze, and kissed him on the cheek.

"I know, Greg. I guess just leave it on until we can get someone here to look at it. I'd call Bob, but he hasn't texted me back, and you know how he gets when you try to talk to him while he's *busy*." She made her way to the laundry room.

"I guess it's going well," Mr. Johnson called back to her. The laundry room door muffled his voice and the presenters on the TRID shopping network.

Mrs. Johnson heaved the hamper onto her cleaning

counter, then turned her attention to the front-loading washing machine. She pressed 'On,' but instead of the normal LED screen showing the estimated washing time, words scrolled along like the news anchor banners. She read them out loud.

"Replace me?" she said. Then the message prompted *Yes or No.* Mrs. Johnson turned the dial to no. The washing machine shook side to side like a toddler when denied a new toy. After a few-seconds fit, the same message scrolled along the screen: *Replace me.* This time, she turned it to yes. A number scrolled across the screen.

Mrs. Johnson dialed it on her cell phone, and after a couple of rings, someone picked up.

"Hello. Thank you for calling the TRID shopping network hotline. Is this Abigail Johnson?" the woman said.

"Yes. How do you—"

"I see your washing machine is acting up."

"Excuse me? This seems like an invasion of my privacy."

"Oh, sorry, ma'am. Our legal counsel has actually advised us that US citizens don't have any right to privacy regarding appliances. So, while this feels like an invasion, it's more—"

Mrs. Johnson hung up her phone and stormed into the living room.

Mr. Johnson was on the couch and leaning forward, the same way he watched his sports games. However, the TRID channel was still on.

"Greg, you'll never believe what just happened to me," Mrs. Johnson said.

Mr. Johnson took a deep breath and turned to her with a shocked look on his face. "Honey, I think I just might."

The TRID network showed two scantily dressed

women and a shirtless man between them behind a counter, all of whom were chiseled by God. The women wore deep purple dresses and the man's upper torso was only covered by suspenders and a bow tie around his neck. He clapped then pointed his index fingers at the camera, but it was his rippling abs that caught Mrs. Johnsons' attention. Mr. Johnson was equally entranced by the women's lustful curves.

"Ladies and gentlemen, we have plenty of dishwashers, washing machines, dryers, blow dryers, tile scrubbers, all for sale. These things are selling like hotcakes," he said. When he said hot, the women dropped low and slid a teasing hand up their legs and mouthed *hot*.

At the bottom of the screen was a banner that read, *Don't make a mistake like Abigail and Greg Johnson. Call now!* Mr. Johnson pursed his lips.

"I called the number on the dishwasher screen, and they knew a bit more than I'd like them to."

Mrs. Johnson whipped out her phone and called Bob.

Bob had his eyes closed, trying to imagine he was anywhere but on this cargo plane miles in the air. He took some motion sickness medicine, but it hadn't kicked in yet. Occasionally, he opened his eyes. Scarily, Agents Dawn, Uloso, and Sol crazily chose not to wear seatbelts. Every time the plane hit turbulence, he squeezed the armrests and immediately checked that his safety belts were tight. If Agent Sol hadn't said "Action" once the plane took off, he wouldn't even try to acknowledge people. Suddenly, doing his own stunts seemed like a bad idea.

The plane was ten feet wide and had minimal seats

built into the plane's inner walls. The lights cast an orange glow onto the scratched-up floors and walls. Everything was brown except for the green door that led to the cockpit. The other actors were finishing their planning scene.

"Affirmative. Agent Bob explained to me that he wants to rest his leg, and this is his process," Agent Sol said. Bob nervously nodded close to twenty times to show his agreement. He didn't dare open his eyes. Whenever someone addressed him, he grunted, and if a grunt didn't work, he gave a quick thumbs up with his right hand.

"Great thinking, Agent Bob," Agent Dawn said. "Agent Uloso, make a note to implement seated and eyes-closed therapy for injured agents. So, we've received reports that D.I.R.T. has already made its move. People's appliances are using LED to communicate the phone number for the TRID shopping network. Our top analysts are trying to figure out the connection between D.I.R.T. and TRID, but no leads so far."

Bob made a mental note. The connection seemed kind of obvious, but he probably revealed it right before the final showdown so the climax could have a two-pronged attack. Agent Sol had given him some pointers before they boarded. They were pretending to be secret agents working for a top-secret government agency. The agency was so secret that Bob couldn't even tell people about it after they finished filming, or he'd be locked away for treason. A little strange, but it worked.

Bob's specific role was to play the surprising recruit who changed up the agency with his uncanny, once-in-a-lifetime gift for agent work. Additionally, Agent Sol confirmed he was indeed the main character. The person in charge of the movie was so impressed with Bob's acting during the initial scene that they made him the main character. Bob's coaches would be so proud. He couldn't wait to tell his parents, but he forgot his phone in the briefing room and couldn't remember the code.

"You understand, Bob?" Agent Dawn said.

Bob forgot to breathe. He didn't catch any of it, so he just gave a quick thumbs up.

"Amazing," Agent Dawn said. "I've never had an agent understand the entire tactical sequence on their first attempt. Agents Sol and Uloso, you should both learn from Agent Bob."

"Oh, yeah, he's great," Agent Sol said. Bob noticed the sarcasm in her voice.

Someone took a seat next to Bob and leaned in. It was Agent Sol whispering to him.

"Cut. You get some rest, okay, Bob? You did great in that last scene. I'll wake you up when we're ready for the next scene," she said.

He wasn't sure whether he actually fell asleep or existed in semiconscious purgatory, but the trip went by a lot faster after he didn't have to listen to people. In his stress- and drug-induced daze, he heard his fellow actors chatting among themselves. No one broke character. They discussed the finer points on the strategy, threw around some coordinates, and talked about post-operation recovery. Bob just focused on stopping his stomach from hurling its contents onto the plane floor.

It wasn't until a strong wind struck Bob's face that he truly woke up. He felt it everywhere besides his eyes. When he opened them, he realized he was wearing goggles. He was also miles above the earth, an endless green mat with concentrations of brown and gray scratches and some white dots below him. Then everything grew terrifyingly fast into a forest, mountains, and snow-capped peaks.

Bob screamed. He wasn't in character, nor was he prepared for a scene. The wind charged into his mouth and down his throat, forcing him to cough violently.

There was someone on his back.

"Oh, hey, Bob. You're awake!" Agent Sol said.

"You didn't say action!" he said.

"I can't hear you. Maybe just close your eyes!"

"This is bullshit!"

They were going way too fast. Bob had never parachuted before, but he had seen a sports car approach a traffic jam too quickly and this was scarier. Snot ran from his nose and tears pooled in his goggles and stung his eyes. The snot slid down to his upper lip, where the wind gusts swept it off his face, much to Agent Sol's disgust. She let out a couple of scoffs.

There was a yank, then a zip sound and a massive billowing. Bob's momentum jerked backward, and he suddenly shot upright instead of laying parallel to the ground. The fall was much slower. When he looked up, a bright white parachute suspended them in the air. The sun shone directly above them and soaked through the parachute fabric, making it look like the angel it was. They weren't going to die.

"Oh, thank God," Bob said. He took the heaviest breaths of his life, truly appreciating the ability to breathe smooth air. Then his anger returned. "You didn't say action!"

"Yeah, sorry about that, Bob. We...uh...had budget cuts. Budget cuts, yeah. Studio blew too much on that last...uh... scene and wanted to save the rest of it for the final, you know, showdown."

"You can't be serious? How is this saving us money?"

"Well, you see, the pilot worked for someone else and

kicked us off since we couldn't pay more. So, this was the safest way for us to get to the next scene."

"Is this normal? Like, I get we're a TV show, but there can't be that much of a difference between this and movies."

"Oh, yeah, it's the worst," Agent Sol said. Her words had a clunky cadence, like she was figuring out the next one only after she said the previous one. She let out a fake growl. "I hate it!" Then she raised an angry fist in the air.

Bob glanced down. They were falling at a much safer rate, and his adrenaline slowed down too.

"You know," he said, "your personality is super different between scenes and behind the scenes. They're both cool, but you're much more serious when we're on camera."

"Um...thanks?"

"No, no, I didn't mean it as an insult. You're just great at acting."

"Oh...yeah, I really pride myself on being able to convince people."

"Uh, maybe I can convince you to...uh...grab dinner." Bob's tone peaked at the end like he was a teenager dealing with puberty voice cracks. He couldn't see Agent Sol's face, but she definitely laughed.

"Did you just ask me out?"

Bob's face went red, and all the sweat prepared to explode from his pores. "Oh"—he let out a fake laugh— "I was totally joking. I know it's stupid." He let out another fake laugh.

"I wasn't offended or anything like that," Agent Sol said, her laugh slowly fading. "I've just never been asked out while parachuting into a mission—I mean, scene. A scene for a TV show."

"Oh, right, we're on set. I'm so sorry. Just, like, forget I said anything."

"I'll give you an answer if we make it out of this."

Bob repeated her sentence a couple of times in his head. He definitely heard her correctly.

"Um...if?"

"Did I say if? I meant when."

Bob was glad she couldn't see his face because it had drooped like a sad clown. The warnings she said in the hospital recovery room replayed for a bit. These next scenes could be legitimately dangerous, and Agent Sol's whole 'if we live' thing didn't mesh well in Bob's mind. However, he made a promise—one he didn't want to break. Part of it was because he wanted to keep a good reputation in the film industry, but mostly, it was because he made it to Agent Sol.

The two drifted to the ground in silence. Eventually, Bob saw and heard birds and insects going about their business. Their chirping and chittering broke the awkward silence between Bob and Agent Sol. The earthy damp aroma of the forest filled Bob's nostrils with a welcomed change from the odorless sky. When Bob was able to see past the trees' canopy, he cherished the opportunity to see dirt once again, something he'd never been so excited to see and step on.

Agent Sol navigated them to a clearing in the forest and landed them gently on the ground, specifically on a small patch of grass that somehow managed to survive among the trees. Bob did a soft squat to catch some of the downward momentum and then popped back up like it was nothing.

He said, "Thanks for everything. The covering for me, the tips, and you know...the whole getting me safely to the ground after we got kicked out of a plane."

"Yeah, no problem."

"You...you're really calm about that."

"Let's just say it happens to me a lot more than you'd think."

"Really? This happens a lot?"

Agent Sol wrapped up the parachute and tucked it into a light brown backpack, which she hid in a tree.

"Forget about it. Circle up."

She explained the plan. D.I.R.T. headquarters was located on the side of a mountain and had plenty of fortifications. Bob and Agent Sol would dress as cable repairers and enter through D.I.R.T. headquarters' service tunnels. At that point, they'd implant a virus into D.I.R.T.'s IT systems, allowing the C.L.E.A.N. analysts to hack in and figure out where they were keeping Director Veritably. It was too late to prevent his codes from falling into the wrong hands, but he could still help stop D.I.R.T.'s operations.

Agent Sol reached into one of her cargo pant pockets and pulled out two plastic tubes about the length of a hand and no wider than a silver dollar. She casually tossed one to Bob then twisted open hers. The top came off with a quiet hiss, and she pulled out a cable repair uniform. Dark blue navy collared shirt, khaki pants, and a hat. Each part of the outfit was pristine, wrinkle-free, and had the warm starchy smell of something recently dry-cleaned. Bob seethed once more at the thought that whoever was in charge spent money on overly elaborate costumes but couldn't secure the actors transportation to the next scene. Whatever...

Bob opened his tube and slipped behind a tree to change.

Once they were both in uniform, Agent Sol took point as they headed north along a poorly maintained dirt path, including numerous jagged tree roots Bob tripped on and piles that Bob incorrectly believed were tiny blackberries.

"We're almost to the scene. Okay? I'll let you know when we start filming," she said.

"Oh, thank God. Honestly, I'm surprised you're not directing this. You're the only person I've seen taking charge this entire time."

She laughed and sighed. "I'm definitely getting a promotion out of this. Don't you worry about me."

Soon, D.I.R.T. headquarters came into view. It was a conspicuous, rusted, cold building that rested awkwardly on a rock plateau, a steep cliff serving as the precarious entranceway just like the old spy movies Bob watched as a kid. It was a little cliché. The face of the building had the same number of vertically barred windows on each side. Another cliff jutted out above it, and gigantic pieces of thunderbolt-shaped tinfoil hung from the edge. Bob stared in disbelief.

"They can't be serious with that," he said.

"Nope, they're serious. It's so when people visit at night, it always looks like it's thundering. Such tools."

Distracted by the hideout and relentless mosquitos buzzing in his face and sucking his blood, Bob couldn't see a path up to the front door at first. Then, once they were much closer to the bottom of the mountain, they stumbled upon a paved road leading into it through a tunnel large enough for two dump trucks to fit side by side. The top of the tunnel read *Service Entrance*. Bob traced the road in the other direction until it vanished into the forest. Ahead lay a bright yellow poster on the left side of the tunnel that read, *For service providers and employees only. All victims and applicants please proceed to the main entrance.*

Agent Sol said, "Come on, Bob. They're waiting for us on set."

Bob perked up and jogged after her and into the tunnel.

He smelled the tunnel first. It was a gross cocktail of rancid food and spoiled milk. Above were unending rows of lightbulbs connected with exposed wires that illuminated the tunnel in an off-white light. The majority of the tunnel's floor was taken up by a cracked and worn paved road with a faded yellow line down the middle separating the lanes. with defaced and dirty grey sidewalks running parallel to the road. Bob tried to hold his breath so he wouldn't smell whatever was coming from the strange liquid that ran along the curb and out of the tunnel.

"This is the way they get actors on set?" Bob said.

"Yeah, acting is a lot tougher than people believe. It's not always helicopters and sandy beaches. And this is actually one of the easier breach points I've had—that's code for the way actors get on set."

"Oh, thanks!" There were so many acting phrases that were niche. It also sounded like something an actual agent would say. He mouthed the words to get into character. "Breach point. Sit rep. Target." Then he pressed his hands together to make a gun and pointed in various directions. Bob was starting to feel it—the excitement of operating beyond the law and completing a mission by any means, regardless of the costs or the collateral damage. That's how a true spy worked.

As he aimed his imaginary gun deeper into the tunnel, something twinkled under the yellow tunnel lights. Bob said, "Hey, Agent Sol, careful of that—"

Crash! A metal portcullis plunged down from the ceiling and in front of Agent Sol. Bob ran forward, grabbed her by the slack on her shirt, and yanked her out of the way. The sharp edges plummeted through the pavement with a sickening crunch, an inch from Agent Sol's foot.

"This set design is ridiculous! How are people supposed

to work under these conditions?" Bob said. He looked at Agent Sol, who sat on the sidewalk, catching her breath.

She looked up at him with wide eyes. "Oh, it's crazy, alright. Thanks for the save. Whew! Okay, let's figure out what's going on," she said and took a breath.

While they were distracted, a second portcullis crashed down behind them. They were trapped. Bob walked over to the first one and tried to give it a yank. "This must be for our chase scene. I'm guessing we have one of those. When we hit the wire, we'll be going so fast, it will close just behind us."

"Oh, right, I forgot. The chase scene...for our comedy," she said with a distant voice. Her eyes fixed on the gate that came down and the silver fishing wire that ran from either side of the tunnel. Agent Sol grabbed hold and traced it back into the wall, where it vanished into a crack between two rocks. "We have to get out of here."

"Let's just call the director or the set design team. Can't they undo whatever is going on?"

"Nope, budget cuts...and they're on strike. Had to cut the whole design team. Bare bones crew and stuff."

"You're joking. Please tell me you're joking."

Agent Sol pursed her lips and frowned, which was followed by a headshake. Bob sighed and started yelling for help.

Moments later, a screen gradually descended from the ceiling with a mechanical whine. The screen flicked on and showed a familiar-looking person around Bob's age, but with a skinny face, curly brown hair, and freckles. He wore the same uniform as the D.I.R.T. actors from the last scene. Bob scratched the back of his head, then he remembered.

"Ned? Ned!" Bob shouted. "I was going to text you later! What are you doing here?"

Ned's jaw dropped. His palms crashed against his cheeks, and he started chuckling. He said, "Holy cow! Bob Johnson? How you been, man! You still playing the saxophone?"

"Oh, I wish. Not anymore," he said. Bob gestured to the logo on his collared shirt. "I actually got into acting. I'm pretending to be a cable security guy." Bob couldn't see, but Agent Sol looked like she wanted to kill him.

"Oh, you, Bob. Always the class clown. How are your parents?" Ned said.

Bob shrugged his shoulders. "Same old, same old. They're still at the same place and both retired. Trying to get into some yacht club."

"Any chance it's Still Rivers?"

"Yeah! That's the one!"

"You won't believe this, but my parents are actually members. Let me text them right now. They can be your recommendations!"

"You'd really do that? Thanks!"

"Of course. Give me a second." Ned turned his attention to something offscreen. Seconds later, Bob heard the whoosh of a sent text message. "Oh, wow, this is awesome. I never expected to see you here," Ned said.

"Right? Same! I didn't think you'd get into acting," Bob said with outstretched arms.

"You know me. I'm *pretending* to be a bad guy." He gestured into his own uniform. "Is she with you?"

Bob turned back and pointed. "Oh, her, yeah, her name is —"

"Action!" Agent Sol said.

"...Your name is Action?"

"Oh, no, sorry. That's Stephanie. She's with me. We heard you guys were having some connectivity issues."

Hopefully, Agent Sol would be okay with that as her alias.

"Okay, cool. We were worried you guys were government spies, but that's clearly not the case. So, you're gonna take this tunnel down until you reach a pink door. Password is unhygienic."

The portcullis cranked up and disappeared into the ceiling. Agent Sol gestured for Bob to come along as she headed into the tunnel.

"Actually, Bob, can you come back here?" Ned said.

Agent Sol stared daggers at Bob and shook her head. She mouthed *no*. Bob looked back and forth between her and the back of the monitor. Ned kept repeating himself. Bob sighed and walked back in front of the TV.

"What's up?" he said.

"You'll never believe it, but Charlie is actually running this whole thing."

"Oh, damn, really? He's the director? Good for him! My mom said he got a huge promotion, but I didn't know it was for this!" Bob said.

He suddenly remembered hanging at Ned's house and Charlie giving them cool new games to play or showing them what cool thing he was up to. It wasn't until now that he realized how distant they had gotten. It hurt to think that Charlie got his huge opportunity and didn't tell him. Also knowing Charlie was the director quashed some of his frustration, though it was strange that he was so irresponsible with the budget. Charlie was usually on top of things like that.

"Yeah, my parents are so proud of him. Well, make sure to stop by and say hi! He'd really love to see you," Ned said.

"Definitely! Thanks for the heads up," Bob said. He waved goodbye, then jogged up to catch Agent Sol. The screen's hydraulics echoed as they pulled the screen back into the ceiling. Once it cleared, Agent Sol snatched Bob's wrist and pulled him in. For a split second, Bob thought she was going to kiss him. Instead, she growled.

"Oh, sorry for breaking character," Bob said.

"Ah, forget that. How do you know that guy?"

"Ned?"

"Yes! Ned. The guy that's gonna get your parents into some stupid club."

"You don't have to be rude..."

"Now's not the time!"

"Okay! Geez. Ned Lorox. He was my best friend back in the day."

"And his brother...."

"Charlie."

"You grew up with Charles Lorox? I said Agent Lorox several times, and you never mentioned that you guys knew each other."

Bob cocked his head back.

"Are...are we still in the scene? Because Agent Lorox is a made-up character for a show. Me...I– Bob Johnson know a Charlie Lorox."

Agent Sol shoved Bob back and pressed her fingers to her eyes.

"Cut. Damn it. This was a mistake." She pulled out her phone and raised it up. "I can't even call for backup. We're in too deep. Damn it!"

Crack! Agent Sol hurled her phone at the wall, and it shattered.

"Hey—what is your first name?" Bob said.

"Lila."

"Okay, it was just getting weird calling you by your character name. Anyway, like I said, I know Charlie. I've had pizza at his house like hundreds of times growing up. Let's get up there. I can talk to him and get things sorted out."

"Bob, you don't get it. Agent Lorox is a bad person! He coordinated and led the attack on C.L.E.A.N."

"So, he's a director that's in his own production. It's a little narcissistic but not unheard of."

"Bob, this isn't a movie!"

"Yeah! I know."

Agent Sol stumbled backward like his words hit her.

"What do you mean, you know?"

"I know this is just a TV show. Might just be some thirty-minute episode that the network throws in the trash. But it also might be a series. Either way, this is my chance to prove myself. So many people are counting on me. My parents, my coaches and mentors, Moni, both Dawn and Veritably. Look, I'm gonna be honest with you. I'm almost thirty. I gave up my career to try this out, and I have nothing to show so far. This is it. Everything for me and everyone I care about is riding on this. So please, I need you to trust me. We can pull this off."

Lila wiped away a tear that made it halfway down her face. She gave a couple quick sniffles and said, "You're right. Everyone's counting on us. We can't turn back now."

Bob smiled and gave an awkward thumbs up, where his expression was a bit too staged. Lila recoiled then laughed. They headed down the tunnel. Lila was quiet the whole way. Her mind was somewhere else, like there was a hamster running on hyper speed in her head. At one point, she asked for Bob's phone and mashed the calculator app's buttons. She mumbled some stuff to herself and bit her lip a few times. When she wasn't looking, Bob smiled. He really hoped they could stay in touch even if the show bombed and she didn't want to date. Lila was super cool.

They reached the pink door and Lila handed back Bob's phone.

"Before we go in, let's go through it one more time," she said. Bob nodded and repeated the steps.

It was a two-step plan. First objective: Upload the virus then wait for HQ to respond. Second: Prepare for the rescue op and extraction. Once they were back at C.L.E.A.N., that would be a wrap on shooting for the day. Bob internally cheered. He hoped Moni was having an equally fun time.

* * *

Moni was back home already. She had started a brand-new gang in the next scene, which took place at an abandoned school. Director and Linda McCarthy, who was strangely wearing Bob's sweater, complimented her for her dedication. Right before she led her gang of post-apocalyptic-looking lunchroom workers to war against the actors, everything in the kitchen started acting up. After that, the actors, Linda, and Director got all weird and sent the extras home. Moni checked her phone, but Bob hadn't responded yet. Then all the cleaning appliances in her apartment started acting up. Moni worried for a moment then remembered that she had eaten some pot brownies. It was all probably in her head.

Chapter Nine

"Action," Lila said, her voice ringing in Bob's ears like a starting gun.

Bob pulled out a pair of sunglasses from within his cable repair uniform and slowly slipped them on.

"Unhygienic," Bob said to the ominous pink door standing before him.

A small slide window opened and dark menacing eyes gazed through. Bob put more strength into his smolder. The two pairs of eyes, Bob's and the stranger's, stared intensely in a war of wills. The first to blink would lose. Bob could feel his eyes aching. The burden of staying open this long was too much. Then the sweat began. Beads sprinted down his forehead and vanished in his eyebrows. One bead navigated through and smashed into an eyelash. It seeped down and stung his eye. Bob squeezed his fist. He would not lose. His opponent was also showing fatigue. The stranger's eyes twitched and vibrated, begging to blink or look in another direction. Then both Bob and the stranger groaned. Their volumes rose into a full yelling match like they were powering up in an anime.

Agent Sol pulled out a folded-up clipboard from her pockets. She slipped underneath Bob and out of view of the stranger. She violently started fanning him, Bob's loose hair rising up like there was a hurricane below him. She aimed her other hand at a nearby light. Her watch fired a red beam, and the light above them turned yellow. Now Bob's hair levitated and looked golden.

Bob smirked. He said, "You have no chance of winning," then went back to yelling. His eyeballs pounded. The sweat stung. His skull ached. Then the stranger blinked. Bob closed his eyes slowly to savor his victory. He gave Agent Sol a discreet thumbs up. When he opened his eyes, the stranger gave him a nod.

He said, "What's your business here?"

"We're here for"—Bob took off his glasses—"fiber optic repair."

The menacing eyes suddenly became friendly.

"Oh! You're Ned's buddy. Great, come on in."

There were a bunch of clicks, some chain rattling, and a metallic groan. Then the pink door swung open. The stranger guided them down a rounded, brick ceiling hallway, which was rough and jagged from the bricks not lining up and so narrow that Bob could almost reach wall to wall and touch the ceiling. The exposed-wire aesthetic continued down this hallway and was just bright enough for Bob to see water dripping from the ceiling and down the walls. About every five or six feet, the water collected into murky puddles, which smelled as putrid as they looked.

Bob kept up with his smolder, which involved not looking down. So even when he stepped into the cold puddles, he didn't dare break character.

The brick hallway ended at another pink door. They went through and suddenly were in some place that looked like a high-tech mall. Specifically, they were standing at the end of a hallway. A glossy eggshell floor stretched out ahead to another dead-end hallway with some signs for bathrooms. Halfway between the two ends was a wall of glass doors, leading to what Bob assumed was the front entrance he saw earlier, and an opening to the rest of the place

"Okay, so you turn right over there, and it's going to open into the atrium. You're gonna take the left escalator to the third floor, then turn left. There's a yellow door with black dots and that's where IT will let you in. We really appreciate the help. Thanks so much for showing up so fast. Also, definitely stop by the gelato bar and let them know Mike sent you. They'll give you extra sprinkles."

With a wave, Mike vanished back into the tunnel. Bob and Agent Sol followed the directions but took a moment after the first right turn. The atrium was a wide, sleek space. In the center was a fountain, the spout being two cherubs each with one arm extended into the air. Stainless steel escalators with beautiful beige handrails carved into the shape of ivy stood on either side. The atrium reached up four stories and culminated with a stained-glass window above. The stained glass showed a scene of untamed nature and a genderless deity staring down at them.

The gelato bar was on the other side of the fountain. The two people behind the counter—a redheaded fair-skinned woman with freckles and a black-haired tan man— waved once they noticed him looking. Bob wanted to wave back and enjoy some gelato, but Agent Bob was on a mission, and they were still shooting.

"Bob," Agent Sol said, "you get lost already? Mike said up the escalator, third floor, yellow polka dot door."

Bob snapped back to reality. "Sorry!" They headed up.

The area was busy. As they rode the escalator, they

passed various hallways that extended off like tree limbs. Various actors in white suits and extras dressed in plain clothing walked from room to room. Some carried prop weapons, some coffee. All of them had stained clothing, from large circles from spills to small blemishes from using their outfits as napkins.

As the fountain's babble faded, the murmur of everyone chatting filled the atrium. Some waved at Bob and Agent Sol. When Bob saw Agent Sol wave to them, Bob figured it was safe for his character to wave as well. So, he did but never dropped the smolder. Once his face was sore, he looked down and dropped the smolder for a few seconds. There was no way they had cameras on the escalator steps.

The third floor was just as elegant as the ground floor. The glass balcony was minimalistic, only having the occasional plant or stainless-steel trashcan neatly tucked against a wall or along the balcony barrier. It was in the shape of an oval that looked straight down to the ground floor. From the balcony, several hallways breached out. Some looked like they were just dead ends, but others looked like they connected with unseen passages. Agent Sol took point to the left, and they followed the rest of Mike's directions to the yellow polka dot door.

Bob opened it up and said, "We're here to help with the internet issues."

The room was square. Tall black servers with blinking lights lined the left wall, and cluttered cabinets lined the right. The cabinets had papers sticking out of the top, and some drawers were partially open. Straight ahead was a wall covered in flyers, sticky notes, and some framed posters with motivational phrases. Below it were several unattended computers and a woman in a desk chair, who spun around.

"Oh, great!" the woman said with a mousy voice. She

had a pixie haircut, hazel eyes, and a nose piercing. The woman wore a sleeveless green dress shirt with a V-shaped neck hole, but then just wore athletic shorts that reached to about mid-thigh. Both of her arms had sleeves of tattoos.

"Servers are right there," she said. "Cabinets have any extenders, ethernet, and caps you guys might need. I'm going to go get some gelato. Call me if you need anything." She got up from her seat and tossed them a radio.

Agent Sol closed the door behind the woman as she left. She started pulling stuff from her pockets and laying it out on the woman's desk. "Okay, Bob, how about you organize those cabinets, so the IT woman will have an easier time finding stuff."

"Consider the case—folder—no, that's not...." He couldn't think of a clever line and so defeatedly said, "I'll get it done."

There were a lot of drawers. To the average person, this was easily a two-person job. However, Bob loved to organize. He put on his sunglasses and looked into the camera.

"Dealing with this must be sort-ture. Time to file-ly fix this."

He nailed it. Bob ignored Agent Sol's groan and got to work. One part of the first drawer had employee records, but also property taxes. He pulled everything out and set up piles and organized each person alphabetically and the property tax bills by property type, assessment date, and amount paid.

"Okay, Bob," Agent Sol said. "I just finished up. However, it—Bob, what are you...You really are doing this, huh?"

"Oh, yeah, I mean, if I'm going to organize something, might as well do it right. What I don't get though is why all this is in the IT room. It seems like an HR or accountant set of files."

"This is a D.I.R.T. facility. They thrive on chaos and disorganization," she said.

"So that's why you wanted me to organize the files. You're amazing!"

He cranked it into overdrive. Bob became a tornado of paper sorting. Folders, files, and boxes swirled in the air as Bob sorted them and they fell into their respective pile.

The door opened, and the mousy woman stood in the doorway with a spoon of gelato in her mouth and several new gelato stains on her clothing. She slowly took out the spoon and said, "You...you guys have been busy." Her gaze slowly turned to the mountains of boxes and papers Bob had sorted. Bob's heart raced. He wasn't sure if the mousy woman caught them, but then again, this must be part of the script. Everything would be fine.

"Yes, sorry, things got a little crazy here," Agent Sol said. "We called the office, and they asked us to confirm some info we thought might be in those cabinets."

"Uh-huh."

"Look, to be honest, I'm just trying to get my cheese and go home. I never know why the bigwigs ask us for the stuff they ask," Agent Sol said.

Bob looked back and forth between them. He didn't remember a call, so they must be trying to convince this D.I.R.T. IT woman that this was all part of their plan. He cleared his throat.

"If I can step in here," Bob said. He reached out with an extended hand and started talking like a mechanic. "Yeah, so, given the remote location of the facility, on the original install, we set up a dedicated light fiber reset line to make sure we could easily pinpoint your switch points and breakers if work had to be done. It helps us trace your connection from end point to end point and diagnose whether it's an internal or structural issue, the latter being a big ol' nightmare. The geniuses over at HQ didn't send us in with the proper IP address and fiber reset line number, and you know, you were so excited about that gelato we didn't want to bother you, so we thought we might find those numbers in your files here." Bob gave a couple foot taps onto the cabinets. "No luck though, but looks like you're back to help us." He smiled.

The woman ate another spoonful of gelato and looked at Bob. She stuck the spoon back into the cup, wiped her hand against her pants and walked past them to the wall of sticky notes, one of which she pulled from the wall and handed to Bob. With the gelato still in her mouth, she spoke, splattering slimy flecks of her partially digested gelato onto Bob's face.

"Here you go," she said. "I'll get out of your hair. Just radio me when you're all done, or if you guys want me to run you up some." She gestured to her bowl and then walked back out.

"Cut," Agent Sol said. Bob started stretching and did some squats. "Bob, what was that? I thought you were an extra."

"Well, actor now." He chuckled. "That career I told you about? I was a software engineer and specialized in internet connectivity and software diagnoses applications."

Agent Sol poorly smothered a chuckle and smiled.

"You're just a wild person, Bob." She walked over to the woman's desk and scooted in on the chair. Her fingers started typing away at the keyboard. "Okay, so for our next scene, you keep doing that while I get ready to receive the location of Director Veritably."

"I mean, can't they just tell us now? They put him there."

"Tsk, tsk. This way we can get more into character. *Agent* Bob wouldn't know—and to really sell this performance, Bob shouldn't know either. Now, action."

Bob returned to his sorting, and Agent Sol focused on the computer in front of her. As Bob closed the last organized cabinet and admired his completed work, Agent Sol called out and said, "Okay, begin operation rescue."

Chapter Ten

A gent Sol pulled a piece of paper from the wall and wrote, *Be back in twenty. Do not enter.* After she posted the note on the outside of the door, the two made their way to the fourth floor then snaked along various hallways. The walls were a smoky gray that worked with the deep purple carpet to create a mismatching but calming atmosphere.

They stood out, clothing-wise, but no one really paid much attention to them. The background actors talked about D.I.R.T. but also last night's game and weekend plans. A couple of people were talking about their book club. It was a little unprofessional to talk about their personal lives during a scene, but Bob couldn't break character to ask them to stay on topic. Charlie would have to deal with that.

He spotted a planter, scooped up some dirt, and rubbed it into his clothing to blend in. Agent Sol didn't notice, but Bob didn't want to disturb her.

Agent Sol stopped in front of a plain wooden door. There was a gold plaque in the center of it that said *Holding*

Cell. Bob frowned. It was a little on the nose and poor set design. Agent Sol and Bob stepped in.

The room was cement gray all around except for the black vertical bars that formed the actual holding cell. The only other person in the room was Director Veritably. He was lying on a messy cot, which was suspended from the wall by a metal chain. He stared emptily at something to Bob's left, something so entrancing that he didn't notice Bob and Agent Sol enter. Bob looked left and gasped.

Lying on the floor was Veritably's jacket covered in wine, red sauce, and mustard stains. Next to it were the remains of his pants trimmed back to the length of shorts with a messy, uneven hem. The worst was his white shirt. The armpits were yellowed, and someone had taken a Sharpie to it and doodled all over it. Agent Sol stumbled back and caught herself on the wall.

"Those...monsters," she said. "Agent Bob, we need to get him out." She shook the gate, but it didn't budge. She searched the room and riffled through a cherry desk in the corner. After a minute, she looked up, frustrated.

"Bob, I can't find the key. It's supposed to be here."

Bob did a quick survey and didn't see it.

"I'm on it," he said. Agent Sol said something to him, but he was out of the room too fast and didn't catch it. Bob walked to the next door labeled *Site Development,* knocked, then opened the door. It was a normal-looking office, desk in the middle, a few windows along the back wall. A brunette woman with a bob cut, doe eyes, a backward baseball cap, leather jacket, and pink ruffly blouse sat at the desk. She looked up with a warm smile.

"Hi," Bob said. "Lila and I were looking for the key, but I think someone forgot to leave it for us."

"Oh, hey there!" the woman said in a Canadian or Minnesotan accent. "What key are you talking about?"

"The holding cell key? Charlie told Lila that it should be there, but we can't seem to find it."

"Oh, I'm so sorry about that," she said with both her hands over her heart. She reached into her pockets and handed Bob a key. "Please take mine. Just bring it back when you're done, okay? Can't have these falling into the wrong hands, don't you know?"

"You are so right. Thank you so much..."

"Jessica." She smiled.

"Thank you, Jessica. I'll be right back."

"You take care now!"

When Bob returned to the holding cell, Agent Sol looked at him with burning eyes, but they extinguished when Bob tossed her the key.

"How did you get this?"

"This lady over in site development. She was super nice. She just gave me the key when I let her know that they forgot to put it in the scene. Oh, wait, sorry. I broke character." Bob looked around for cameras and said, "Sorry, everyone. Can we start from the top?"

While Bob apologized, Agent Sol unlocked the cell and rushed to Director Veritably.

"Director!"

Veritably snapped out of his daze. He rubbed his eyes then perked up after seeing Agent Sol and Bob. "Agent Sol? Agent Johnson? Oh, I can't believe it's you. What's going on? Why are you here?" He seemed so out of breath and worn after each sentence. When he tried to lift himself off the cot, his arms and legs trembled. He was really selling the role!

"Director," Bob said in his gravelly voice, "the current

operation is a recovery and extraction op. We've identified the egress point and are prepared to execute on your order."

Agent Sol sighed and said, "Yeah, what he said."

Director Veritably eventually got to his feet, but his muscles wouldn't stop shaking.

"Perfect. Let's execute and then we can figure out how to stop D.I.R.T."

Bob nervously tapped his foot. They were having a wonderful moment, but he had to get the key back to Jessica. He could probably just drop it off on their way to the next scene. The office was on the way.

"We need to move. We only bought enough cover for twenty minutes," Bob said. "If we don't hurry, they're going to *clean* our clock."

Veritably nodded.

"You're right, Agent Johnson. Let's go. We've lost too much on this mission. Let's get ourselves a win." He looked sadly at his black suit and shirt.

Agent Sol supported Veritably as he walked. Bob asked for the key back.

"You can't be serious?" she said.

"A true agent never goes back on a promise," Bob said.

"Dang it, Bob, you never cease to impress me. When we get back, you're getting that promotion," Director Veritably said before giving in to a forceful cough. Bob smiled. That sounded like he was getting invited to another filming, and it was going to be either another season or maybe a spin-off. Either outcome was awesome.

"Fine, whatever," Agent Sol said. "But give me the extra disguise in your lower left pant pocket."

Bob reached in and pulled out a couple more capsules and handed them to Agent Sol.

Bob exited the room first and swung by Jessica's office.

He stood in the doorway as Director Veritably and Agent Sol limped past him.

"Hey, Jessica, thanks again. We just finished up what we needed. Really appreciate the help," he said, tossing the key to her.

"Oh, don't you worry one bit! You take care now, you hear?" Jessica said. She caught the key and gave a wave as Bob jogged to catch up with his fellow actors.

"Agent Sol," Bob said, "do you think we need to take down that sign we left at the IT room?"

"No, don't worry about that," she said. "The set team will take care of that."

Director Veritably looked at Agent Sol and raised an eyebrow. Agent Sol then whispered something in Veritably's ears. His eyes went wide, and he stared at Bob.

Bob was a little uncomfortable. They had to be talking about him. However, Director Veritably ended up smiling approvingly at Bob, so it probably wasn't anything negative. He made a mental note to ask Agent Sol what it was about just to be sure.

They made it back out to the atrium, where a wall of D.I.R.T. actors greeted them. Bob didn't recognize them, but he recognized Charles Lorox standing in front. He looked like a scarred but polished version of his high school self. Charles had the same dark brown crew cut that led right into his five o'clock shadow.

"Well, well, well," he said. "Agent Sol and—Bob? What are you doing here with these people?"

Bob froze. He was so conflicted. They were in a scene, but here was the director breaking the fourth wall. He looked to Agent Sol for guidance, but she didn't take her eyes off the D.I.R.T. actors.

"I...uh..." Bob said then looked at Charles, or *Charlie*.

He wasn't sure who should take the lead, Bob or Agent Bob. No one else was breaking character. The D.I.R.T. actors still had their prop guns aimed at the three of them. Veritably still looked like he could collapse any second. Agent Sol still had her processing look. Even all the background actors went about their business like none of this was happening.

"Cat got your tongue?" Charles Lorox said. "Ned told me you were in the building, so I've been trying to find you to say hi before I had to step out for an operation, but then my VP told me someone requested the key to Veritably's cell. You can't believe my surprise to find it was you."

Bob bit his lip. Was this part of the scene? If he played a character with the same backstory as his real-life backstory, then all of this would make sense. If this wasn't part of the plot, Charles should already have known Bob was here. After all, he was the director and had to know who was playing his main character. So that had to be it. He was playing an agent version of himself; Ned was playing an evil henchman version of himself, and Charlie was playing an evil villain version of himself. That was the only thing that made sense.

"You know why I'm here," Bob said, turning on his smolder. "We're here to save the director."

"Why did your voice drop, and why is your face like that?" Charles said.

Bob's confidence broke again as he spiraled into self-doubt. The D.I.R.T. actors standing behind him turned the safeties off their prop guns.

"Agent Lorox," Agent Sol said.

"Don't call me that!" he yelled. Charles drew a pistol and held it up to Agent Sol, who didn't flinch.

"The unidentified agent," she said through gritted teeth, "is the result of a compromised pre-operation engagement and lacks the prerequisite knowledge to fully appreciate the current situation."

Charles burst into laughter. He laughed until he almost fell down, but one of the D.I.R.T. actors moved over a couch to catch him.

"Bob, do you have any idea what's going on? Bob–you, Bob, not whatever you're pretending to be," Charles said after his laugh eased.

Bob looked down at his collared shirt. "A cable repair...person."

"Wow. You really think you're an agent," Charles said. "You're really committed to this thing. The scruffy voice, the action-star squint and smolder, the whole nine yards."

Bob looked to Agent Sol and silently asked *Cut*. She sighed and shook her head.

"Oh, wait, you have an activation word. What did you mouth? Cut? Yeah, cut!" Charles said.

Bob let out a sigh of relief.

"Thanks for that. You have no idea how confused I was. First, I was like, 'Oh, it's the bad guy,' and then you were like, 'Oh, it's my brother's friend,'" Bob said.

"Yeah, sorry about that. You can ignore everyone back there, okay? This is just like a mini-cut." He pointed to everyone going about their business behind him and the D.I.R.T. actors holding prop rifles.

"Okay, well, if we have a break," Bob said. He cleared his voice and then stormed up to Charlie. "Dude, what are you thinking?" He caught Charlie off guard, and Charlie leaned back on the couch. "How are you going to throw me out of a plane and walk through a sketchy service tunnel because of budget cuts, then have this insane set design? There's what, a hundred extras? You can have half the amount and just have them change clothes. Oh, and a gelato bar with real gelato! That's insane! Then don't even get me started on this plot. My God, D.I.R.T. and C.L.E.A.N. Do you realize how stupid that is?"

Lila said, "Bob, hang—"

"No, I've held this in for way too long. I got a lot of respect for Charlie and his family, but this is insane. Someone's gotta say something, and it looks like no one else will!" Bob enunciated every word until some people walking around in the back stopped to watch. "You are so much better than this. What happened to the Boy Scout, huh? The guy that would volunteer after practice and on his free weekends or showed me how to ride a bike and do a flip off the jungle gym. What happened to the guy who wanted to help the world? I refuse to believe that he became the director of bad TV shows." Bob took a step back and crossed his arms. "Now, I'm done. Actually, hang on, I'm not done yet. Can you direct? Seriously, this entire time I've been improvising. Thank god for Lila. Then the extras! I'm trying to act my butt off, but then we got people planning their fantasy line-up or figuring out what stupid bucket of ice cream is on sale. Like, come on! Is this filming or are we just all hanging out in a secret terrorist facility!"

Bob looked at everyone's faces, and their expressions were consistent across the board. They were shocked. At first, Bob felt bad. He needed to say those things. Charlie was making some serious mistakes with his budget, and no one was telling him. Plus, with a budget this big, Charlie needed good results, but Bob wasn't seeing them.

Charlie stood up and scratched his chin. After chewing on his lower lip, he said, "You know what, Bob? You made a lot of good points."

"Really?" Bob said.

"Yeah," Charlie said, drawing out the word. "This is

what we're going to do. We're gonna have one last scene. Then I'm going to send you home in a private car, and I'll see you later."

"Okay! That sounds like a good plan," Bob said. He gave a quick, nervous laugh. "And look, I'm really sorry. I went too far. It's just—I have bad motion sickness, and there was a lot of moving around with the planes, the horses, the acrobatics, and stuff. It's just all been a lot."

Charlie stared at him for a bit longer, then clapped a hand on his shoulder. In a voice that started nice but devolved into something menacing, Charlie said, "All water under the bridge. So, this is what we're going to do. Director Veritably and Agent Sol are going to play damsels in distress. You have to rescue them both or neither. I don't really care." He pointed to a white suit actress. "Veronica, here, is going to take you to your changing room. You hang out there while I get them set up."

Lila yelled and said, "Bob! Just—"

Click. Charlie turned off the safety of his prop gun.

"Lila, don't interrupt the man's process."

"Charlie, this isn't a—"

"Lila...be a good little actress and stay quiet like Veritably right here."

"I'll be okay," Bob said. "This is all really good motivation. The hero's friends are captured and in danger! I'll see you guys in a bit!"

Bob went along with Veronica, who was not friendly at all. Bob tried to make small talk, and she grunted her responses. After three failed attempts, he decided to just focus on getting ready for the scene.

She opened the door, which revealed an office with lounge seating along the walls, magazines on a little coffee table in the center of the room, and a backwall counter with drinks and snacks. The room smelled sterile like they had transplanted a dentist's waiting room. With one last grunt, Veronica shoved him in, closed the door, and locked it.

Bob sauntered over to the couch and took a seat. He flipped through the magazine options, but none seemed appealing. They also all looked like really elaborate props. One, *Evil Lair Monthly*, had Charlie on the cover. The associated article talked about how Charlie turned a former cult hideout into the D.I.R.T. lair. He tossed it back on the table. Bob sighed. The other options weren't interesting at all. He could either read about the history of paint or about some bougie wedding between a famous food distributor and a self-help book author. Bob was even more down when he remembered he left his phone back in the briefing room.

Bob looked at the clock on the wall and realized he might be late to hang with his friends. He sighed. The life of an actor was demanding.

He adjusted to a comfier spot on the couch and let out a yawn. Bob wasn't sure if he had time for a nap, but it couldn't hurt. He laid down on the couch and closed his eyes.

The door opened, and Bob woke up, startled. He looked at the clock and saw about twenty minutes had passed. Veronica stood in the doorway with a duffle bag and tossed it at him.

"Change," she said. Then she slammed the door shut. She opened it again and said, "Now." She slammed the door again.

He unzipped the duffle bag and found a black suit, just like the one he put on at the Wild West jail earlier that day. This one was fresh, though. He looked at the inside of the jacket and smirked. *C. Lorox* was stitched into the inner lining. Had Charlie played a C.L.E.A.N. agent before? Was this a sequel to one of Charlie's earlier projects? So cool. It was also a cost-saving measure, and Bob appreciated the fact that Charlie took some of his rant to heart.

He sifted through the duffle bag and pulled out something that looked like a glue stick labeled 'Stain Remover', a prop pistol filled with the same cleaning pellets from the hangar fight, extra magazines, and an 'Agent Sized' dental floss container. Based on the floss's subheading, 'Agent Sized' was about a thousand feet. He slipped the tools into various pockets and sat back down. Bob took a deep breath and thought about his mission. Not the mission for the movie, but his life mission. He came here as an extra but was leaving as a main character. His gut tingled. It could open up so many doors for him and his family. He'd be able to focus on getting into shape if a studio picked him up. He'd be able to pull strings and get his parents into that yacht club—oh, wait, Ned said his parents could help with that. Bob didn't actually have that many reasons why he wanted to be an actor.

Bob was suddenly dreading the world where Charlie asked him to star in another season and having to turn it down. It would be really awkward, particularly when he'd have to tell Veritably and Dawn. Even more so when he told Lila.

"Bob, can you hear me?" Charlie said. His voice came through the loudspeaker.

"Yeah?" Bob said, trying to find where he could talk back. They didn't give him a microphone or anything like that.

"Good. Are you dressed for your big performance?"

"Yeah," Bob said shortly. He was annoyed. Bob did a bunch of scenes before this and thought they were mostly good. It was a little insulting to pretend that he hadn't done anything before this.

"Okay, then. Action!"

Agent Bob took over. He put on the smolder, cocked the prop gun, and snickered.

"Time to take out the trash."

Chapter Eleven

ob kicked open the door and it launched off the
hinges, taking out Veronica, who was standing
behind it. Bob rolled into the hallway, recovered in
a squat position, and fired two pellets at the D.I.R.T. actors
sprinting at him.

Pft. Pft. The shots hit their marks, and the D.I.R.T.
actors collapsed to the floor, crying out as the stains
vanished from their outfits. An assailant charged him from
behind, but Bob launched his elbow backward and hit the
person in the stomach. Then, he reached for the assailant's
neck, pulled down, and launched the whole body over his
shoulder.

"Time to separate the goods from the bads."

He stood up and went down the hallway toward the
atrium. There wasn't any resistance for the rest of the way,
but before he stepped out of cover, he examined his situation. It was quiet. Too quiet. He surveyed the shadows
along the balcony. There were way more than he remembered. Bob immediately knew it was an ambush. It was just
like when he was an extra in the western jail cell. Someone

said action. There was a tense silence. The two actors went outside and were immediately in pain. Bob wouldn't do the same. He took out his floss, pulled enough to make a tiny ball, then hurled it out.

Gun shots echoed in the atrium as the lurking, trigger-happy D.I.R.T. actors revealed themselves and decimated the floss ball. Bob had to make it to the escalator to reach the top floor. Villains always kept their final scenes at the top or bottom of their hideouts in the most inconvenient place. He had already seen the bottom levels, so there was nowhere to go but up. Unfortunately, up had a lot of things stopping him.

Bob retreated to his changing room. He used some of the floss to tie couch cushions to the coffee table, and then lifted it up like a shield.

Now prepared, he stepped into danger. The D.I.R.T. actors fired wine projectiles that blasted into the table shield. Every couple of shots, a wine projectile would leak through and run down his hair and past his nose, leaving the smell of sour grapes and dirt, the mark of a clearly cheap vintage. The barrage quickly tore away at his table shield, but it lasted enough for him to slide into the safety between the escalator railings. Bob pressed his back against one railing and caught his breath. There were at least fifty enemies on the top floor and only one of him. This was going to be an awesome scene.

He pulled out his prop pistol and fired some pellets. There were too many enemies and not enough ammo to take them all out that way.

Pft! A wine projectile whizzed an inch over his head and crashed into the escalator railing behind him. He had to come up with a diversion. He scanned the ceilings and spotted fire extinguisher nozzles. Once one was about thirty yards away, Bob aimed and fired. The first two missed but the third hit with a satisfying *ssssssss* as water burst out of the nozzle in an extreme shower. Water, combined with whatever chemicals were in the pellets, distracted the enemies. One howled.

"There's soap in my eye!" he said.

Bob fired and took out a couple more sprinklers. More water sprayed out, drenching everything on the top level. As Bob ascended, the air became more humid and smelled like stagnant water. He also noticed the top of the escalator, meaning the end of his cover quickly approached. The D.I.R.T. actors' barrage had slowed following the sprinkler stunt but was still too strong for Bob to make it out. If he didn't come up with a solution, he was going to be seriously hurt—and he had a feeling Charlie didn't get actor insurance. He couldn't even retreat because the railings behind him were decimated and would leave him exposed.

There were only a few feet left before Bob was in the D.I.R.T. actors' fire. Three seconds. Bob's eyes desperately scanned around for the next source of cover. Two seconds. Bob's brain frantically scoured every memory for some potential plan. One second. Bob crouched and closed his eyes, still bound by his commitment to stay in character.

Psh! The stained-glass ceiling shattered above Bob. Black suit actors descended from black ziplines connected to helicopters hovering in a purple sky. Leading the charge was Agent Dawn, who wore her blue combat outfit and fired from a prop pistol in each hand. Her voice echoed when she said, "Move it, people! Director, Sol, and Johnson need our help!"

As the black suit actors distracted the D.I.R.T. actors, Bob dashed out to a hallway after he safely arrived on the top floor. He took shelter against the wall and gave cover fire for his descending allies.

There was so much gunfire, a smoky haze filled the fourth floor of the D.I.R.T. headquarters. Director Dawn thudded to the ground and made her way to Bob.

"Agent Johnson, you are one tough son of a gun. What's the situation?" she said.

"Agent Sol and Director Veritably have been captured by the enemy."

"Worse than I thought. The boys at the lab are trying to determine the connection between TRID and D.I.R.T. Once we do that, we can shut this operation down for good."

She tossed him a couple of ammo magazines.

"While Agent Sol and I were hacking into their systems," he said, slipping the ammo magazines into his suit "we realized that TRID is the front. TRID is D.I.R.T. backwards."

"Agent Johnson, you're a genius."

She pulled out her radio and said, "This is Agent Dawn. Agent Johnson figured out the connection. Get Judge Ajax on the line and get a warrant to shut down TRID's operations. They are in league with D.I.R.T." She turned back to Bob. "When this is over, we need to talk about promotions. Now, go save our agents."

Bob nodded, turned on the smolder, and sprinted down the hallway. He followed the trail of wall signs that read *D.I.R.T. Stadium.* Based on Bob's experience with cheesy spy shows and knowing Charlie's love for sports, he had a feeling that the final showdown would take place there.

Two D.I.R.T. actors leaped out from offices. One fired and the wine blast slammed into Bob's left shoulder, sending him stumbling backward. The other actress shot, but Bob threw himself behind cover before it hit. His shoulder ached as the red wine slid down his black suit jacket. He could already feel a bruise coming on right where the wine stain was. It was a miracle the impact didn't break his shoulder.

He poked his head out. Two more shots fired and slammed into Bob's cover. The drywall burst away into a cloud of dust, but not before Bob could see where they were hiding. One was behind a plant, the other behind an open door. He tapped his foot. This was an action scene. He couldn't afford to waste time. Bob wrapped one of his pellets with floss until it was roughly the size of a baseball.

"Grenade!" Bob said, tossing it at his enemies. They yelped. Bob slid to the closer one behind the door. He carried the momentum up and shoulder checked his enemy's cover, the door knocking the D.I.R.T. actor to the ground. Bob fired a pellet into the person's chest, the pellet's contents lifting the stains from the enemy's shirt. He leveraged the new position and aimed at the remaining D.I.R.T. actor. She panicked and ran after she shot at Bob, who avoided the wine projectiles. As the remaining D.I.R.T. actor ran out of the way, Bob fired another pellet. It clipped her ankle and she stumbled to the ground.

Bob shot her wrist as she reached for her prop rifle. She crab-walked away from him.

"Please! Have mercy!" she said.

"Leave the gun and get out of here," Bob said. "Learn how to make every day... brighter." Bob pulled out the glue stick and showed it off to the actress.

She started laughing, which Bob sneered at. It was very unprofessional to break character.

"Oh, right—cut!" the actress said. She reached for her prop rifle again, but Bob fired a pellet before she could grab it. The actress collapsed as the pellet's contents took care of the ketchup stain on her stomach. Bob shook his head. That extra was really unprofessional.

Shortly after, the hallway ended, and the modern and sleek aesthetic came to an abrupt halt, turning into another shoddily built red brick tunnel. It smelled faintly like the warm and ashy scent of fire. There was all a dull chant and cheer that moved through the tunnel which opened into a massive stadium-sized cave, its bench seating built into the surrounding rock.

The top level, where Bob stood, circled the stadium. Four flights of stairs with handrails, evenly spread out around the stadium, ran down to the stadium's pit, which was roughly the size of a small soccer field. Between each set of stairs was a sea of rambunctious attendees, all of whom stared at the dirt floor.

On the left side of the pit, Director Veritably dangled from a crane mounted on the other side of the stadium, over a bubbling in-ground pool of marinara large enough to swallow up a couple of SUVs end to end. He was bound by heavy metal chains wrapped around his arms and torso. On the right side of the pit was Agent Sol inside a ring of violent robot bunnies from the obstacle course.

"Welcome, Bob!" Charles's voice boomed in the stadium. His voice re-energized the crowd. Charles was straight ahead on a platform, about halfway up the stadium. He sat on a black leather throne. Next to his throne was the base of the crane, a D.I.R.T. actor in the operating seat behind a glass wall.

"I'm honestly surprised you made it this far," Charlie said. "But as promised, here are your two fellow agents. At my command, Director Veritably will meet his red end, and Agent Sol will become a dust-bunny in the wind!" He laughed, then the crowd joined in. Charles raised a fist, and everyone went quiet. "You will put your own life in danger. There will be nothing to save you from the horrors of a failed rescue. That being said, you may take off your suit and walk right out. My agents will not attack you if you remove that outfit."

Bob looked at his two comrades in danger. Time was his biggest enemy. Director Veritably would go into the pool at the same time the bunnies attacked Agent Sol. He would have to make it down there, and from the looks of the crowd, they weren't going to make it easy.

"I'll give you one last chance, Agent Lorox. Abandon your evil mission and walk away from all this. We don't need to settle this with violence," Bob said. "Imagine all the good you could do with this creativity and technology. Making the world dirty doesn't need to be your life's mission."

The crowd responded angrily with boos and insults, most of which would probably ruin the show's chance at a TV-PG rating. Then a hush swept over the crowd as Charles stood up and responded.

"What would you know, Bob? You think this is a movie?"

Bob shook his head. Why was he the only one that knew what this was going to be? He took a deep breath and drew his prop pistol.

"Former Agent Lorox... I guess you leave me no choice."

Agent Sol and Director Veritably yelled something, but the crowd drowned them out. It didn't matter since Bob knew the timer started. The bunnies leaped at Agent Sol, who dodged and rolled out of the way. She shed her shirt and wrapped it around her fist as a gauntlet. Director Veritably threw his body weight back and forth until he was swinging. He then thrust his legs in the air so that he hung upside down. He then wrapped them around the chain. Director Veritably climbed the rope with his legs roughly at the same speed that the chain was lowering him. Bob sprinted down the stairs to the cheers and boos of the gathered crowd.

Two D.I.R.T. attendees stuck their feet out to trip Bob, but he vaulted onto the handrail that divided the stairs. Bob slid down to the next landing using his shoes like a skateboard. Another three D.I.R.T. attendees hopped into the aisle with vicious looks. The first threw a hook. Bob hurled his body backward and landed on his hands. He followed the momentum and uppercut the first attacker with his feet. The attacker fell back into the crowd. Bob got back to his feet. The crowd cheered.

The other two lunged. Bob caught one by the wrist, pulled her forward, then chopped at her neck. She dropped. A fist hit his jaw, making him stumble. The third attacker landed another hit to Bob's stomach. Bob doubled over and hit the ground, the stone stairs hurting more than the hit that knocked him down. He recovered in time to catch the attacker's heel.

Bob brought the heel a bit closer to his chest then twisted it. The third attacker lost his balance and tumbled down the stairs. Bob wiped the blood from his lip and continued down, leaping over the fallen attacker. Some more attendees rocketed out, but Bob dodged their attempted blows.

Finally, at the bottom of the stairs, he flipped over the barrier and landed on the dirt field. Sprinting to Agent Sol, Bob fired at the robot bunnies but missed. The bunnies were too quick. Now aware of Bob, some turned and attacked him. He took several steps back and continued firing, still having no luck as they teleported from side to side.

"Agent Sol, to me!" Bob said, putting away his prop gun and pulling out the agent-sized floss box. He danced around the bunnies' assault, some of them landing cuts with their razor fangs. Bob sprinted to the marinara pool and kept pulling out floss, letting the excess trail behind him. He reached the edge of the bubbling hot marinara pool, the heat shimmering in the air.

Director Veritably hung upside down about twenty feet above the surface of the pool. After getting in range, Bob hurled the box of floss at Director Veritably, who snaked one leg around the metal chains and extended the other to catch the box of floss, his body shaped like a "y"

"Go, Agents!" he said.

Bob pulled and pulled the floss as they got closer. It needed to be taut. If it wasn't, he was going straight into the marinara pool. He gulped.

Agent Sol shouted nervously. "What's your plan, Bob?" she said, punching the bunnies. She had almost caught up to Bob, but so had the bunnies, their laser red eyes and cyclone dagger mouths sending a shiver down his spine.

"Do you trust me?" Bob said. He kneeled and tapped his thigh. Agent Sol nodded. Without hesitating, she launched herself off Bob's thigh, going about six feet into the air, and catching the floss rope before falling into the marinara pool. Bob choked up on the string, raised his legs, and turned his body sideways as they swung on the floss rope.

Two things cross Bob's mind. The first was the heat, which seared his back each time the bubbling marinara popped like it was left in the pot too long without being stirred. The second was gratitude for all the planks he did for stunt training. His trainer said planks were an excellent low-impact ab workout and useful for doing your own stunts.

Then a dark thought crossed his mind. Despite his mind begging to hold on, Bob's throbbing, disobedient shoulder weakened. The marinara reached up for him, burning Bob's back as it dug its saucy claws into him.

His shoulder gave in. Bob lost his grip. But right before his shoulder dipped below the surface, a powerful hand reached down, grabbed the fit of his suit, and held him up. His hero, Agent Sol, smiled down at him, her body stretched out as she saved Bob from a hot aromatic end.

As soon as they cleared the pool, Bob let go of the floss and Agent Sol released her grip. The two actors crashed to the earth on the other side of the marinara pit and rolled for a bit as their momentum faded. After catching his breath, Bob looked back. All the bunnies had surged after them and vanished beneath the red, hot surface of the marinara pool. One tiny metal paw stuck out as if waving goodbye before sinking out of sight.

"Damn it!" Charles said, his voice booming through the loudspeakers. "Fine, you get one, but can you save the other?"

The chain descended faster, and Director Veritably had lowered a few feet while holding the floss. Bob pushed himself up to kneel, his abs and left shoulder screaming out in exhaustion. He visually tracked the chain along the shaft of the crane to the operator, who remained behind cover. Bob fired a few pellets, but the glass wall didn't crack. Agent Sol dashed past Bob and snagged the last of the floss before it fell into the marinara.

"Grab on! We can pull him over," she said. Agent Sol wrapped the floss around her hands, and Bob did the same in front of her, relying on his unbruised right shoulder. The two heaved like they were playing tug-of-war against the crane. It was not easy. They were at an odd angle, and the director was made heavier by the solid chains binding him.

"Come on!" Agent Sol said through a groan.

Bob's body was reaching its limit. His arms trembled as he tried to exert more strength. Defeated, his feet slid against the dirt toward the pool as his thighs refused to resist the crane's pull anymore. Bob wanted to end the scene. To get some sort of break before his body completely gave out and he couldn't perform the final chase scene.

With one last heave, Director Veritably landed on the dirt, safe from a saucy grave. In the meantime, Bob collapsed and stared up at the sky. It wasn't a scene break, but he had to. They completed the rescues, which made this a good break point. If Charlie didn't like how Bob was acting, he could yell cut. Bob was too exhausted and in too much pain to care.

"Bob!" Agent Sol said. She sounded worried, but Bob wasn't sure why. She riffled through his jacket pockets and pulled out the stain remover. Quickly, she rubbed the stick all over his exposed skin, then slipped a hand underneath his shirt to apply some to his left shoulder. His skin quickly absorbed the cool, minty lotion. It relieved enough pain that Bob could prop himself up on his elbows.

While he was turning around, Agent Sol undid Director Veritably's chains.

Once freed, he said, "You got a great career ahead of you, kid."

Bob gave an absent nod, still woozy from all his exertion.

"No, no, no!" Charles said through the loudspeakers.

"You're not even an agent! You're just some guy who got on the wrong bus."

Were they still filming? Did Charles yell cut and Bob didn't hear? In the back of Bob's mind, he wondered if there was truth to it. Wouldn't it be wild if he actually ended up in a secret government facility by accident, then got caught up in a world-ending software attack?

"Agent Bob," Agent Sol said, "are you with us? The rescue was a success. Now we need the extraction."

Charles said, "No! Cut—"

"Off our means of exit," Agent Sol said. "You cur! But you're no match for the power of C.L.E.A.N."

"You know what? Screw this. All agents—attack!"

The cheers and boos turned into battle cries as hundreds of D.I.R.T. actors descended from the stadium, an avalanche of white suits and regularly dressed people aimed directly at Bob.

Chapter Twelve

Director Veritably stole Bob's prop pistol and opened fire. "We need a plan to get out of here."

"Up the chains," Agent Sol said. "Agent Bob, you first."

Bob looked at the chain. It wasn't moving anymore. Both the operator and Charlie fled from the platform, out of sight, down a dark corridor behind his throne. Bob nodded and started climbing with his restored strength to the long jib extending from the crane's base. Below was a horde of bloodthirsty D.I.R.T. actors converging from every direction, calling for vengeance.

"Bob! Go!" Agent Sol said.

She followed Bob up the chain, then Director Veritably brought up the rear. Once the chain went horizontal—and with the jib too thin to walk along—Bob slipped under and swung across like they were monkey bars. Once close enough, he rolled onto the platform where Charlie had addressed them, then looked back to catch Agent Sol and Director Veritably. Their enemies rowdily followed them on the chain and were gaining fast. Bob dashed to the crane controls and started the chain descending again, sending the D.I.R.T. actors into the marinara pit.

Agent Sol had her finger pressed against her earpiece and said something Bob couldn't hear. Then she turned to Bob and Director Veritably.

"This way!" she said.

Agent Sol pointed to the well-lit corridor behind Charles's throne. Seconds later, everything started trembling.

"Damn it! He launched the self-destruct. He's taking us all out," Agent Sol said.

Bob instinctually smiled but hid it once he noticed it creeping across his face. This was it. The epic end to filming. He had to nail this, his swan song of a short-lived acting career.

Dust sprinkled from the ceiling in sync with a distant explosion. Thin and jagged cracks formed in the wall and ran across like they were racing Bob to the end of the corridor. Despite the rumbling coming from behind them, Bob stopped to look back. The hallway was collapsing like a rubble wave. His heart jumped, and he sprinted to catch up.

"Collapsing tunnel!" he said. Everyone ran faster.

Within seconds of the corridor collapsing, the three dove out into a new cavern. The new cavern had a natural dome shape, stalactites hanging threateningly above them, ready to fall at any second. Flickering white fog lights mounted on the walls brightened the area, revealing aspects and details of the cavern in brief flashes—except for a vacuum of darkness to the right. Bob stared at the vacuum, a car-sized tunnel so dark it resembled the maw of death itself ready to swallow them whole. Sadly, Bob knew it was the only way out, the word *Exit* in pulsing red light. The cavern was stable for now but wouldn't be forever. The trembling grew stronger with every rumble. Based on Agent's Sol's face, she had the same fears.

"Bob, you ride with me. Director, you take your own bike," Agent Sol said, running to the left to a row of cars and motorcycles. Dust sprinkled from the ceiling. Bob's heart raced as he sprinted after her. Stunts hadn't gone well this entire time, and now didn't seem like the best time to try motorcycles.

"Can we take a car?" Bob said.

"Too slow. Not agile enough," Agent Sol said. She swung her leg over the motorcycle seat and fiddled with the controls until the engine kicked on. The engine's roar bounced off the cavern walls. Cracks ripped open along the walls and ceiling. "Stop wasting time!"

A stalactite broke from the ceiling and impaled the motorcycle next to Agent Sol, who didn't flinch. Bob gulped but listened and mounted the motorcycle. By the time Bob got to Agent Sol, Director Veritably started his own motorcycle.

"You two take point. I'll bring up the rear," he said. He cocked his prop pistol. Bob wrapped his arms around Agent Sol's torso, laid his head against her back, and closed his eyes. He could hear her snicker.

"Doesn't this feel familiar? Just hold on tight, okay? I'm gonna get you out of this," she said. The motorcycle launched forward, speeding down the tunnel.

Vroom! The engine's whine filled their dark surroundings, the only source of light the motorcycle's headlight. Ahead stretched a two-lane road that wound left, right, up, and down. Agent Sol swerved around falling rubble, unphased by the debris that sprayed her face or the haunting sound of the blacktop cracking below them like a cackling monster.

The back tire slipped as a fissure formed perpendicular to the road, separating the tunnel. Bob glanced back to see Director Veritably launching himself off a pile of rubble to jump the gap. The director threw up both hands and shouted something that sounded like *Wheeeee*. His motorcycle landed with a thud and mild swerve, from which he quickly recovered.

They rounded another corner, the setting sun gleaming in from the left side of the tunnel through stone-carved windows and framed by crude stone columns every five feet. The windows gave them a wide view of the outside world, an unending sea of treetops. Soon after they crossed into the orange sunset's light, Bob heard the thumping sound of helicopter blades. Then it shot into view and faced them. It projected Charles' voice.

"You think you can run?" he said. "You think I lost? Think again!" The machine guns mounted to the bottom of the helicopter wound up.

"Incoming fire," Agent Sol said. She swerved to the right side of the tunnel, which Director Veritably copied. The helicopter's machine guns whirled then unleashed a storm of projectiles that devastated the columns and left holes all along the opposite wall making it look like a honeycomb. Bob gripped tighter as Agent Sol drove in random patterns.

"I'm sorry, Bob. Hold on!"

Bob closed his eyes and steadied his breath. His stomach spun in circles, his partially digested food jumping into his throat. Bob took deeper breaths, but it wasn't working. His motion sickness medicine was wearing off, and he didn't have more. It didn't help that every millisecond a bullet tore into something—stone, asphalt, or the exhaust pipes behind his feet.

"Director!" Agent Sol said. "We need to get rid of that thing."

"On it," Director Veritably said. His motorcycle sounded like it was falling back before surging forward and toward the left side of the tunnel. Next came the sound of the motorcycle crashing against the stone wall, then silence as the momentum launched Director Veritably out of the tunnel and through the air directly at the helicopter. His motorcycle plummeted to the earth, but Director Veritably looked like a missile, his arms extended out forward, his legs tucked tightly against each other.

Once the helicopter was close enough, Director Veritably reached out a hand and grabbed onto the helicopter's landing skid. His momentum carried his legs forward and he let go of the skid, launching him to the skid on the other side. Bob stopped breathing as Director Veritably floated underneath the helicopter, the ruthless force of gravity ready to break Director Veritably against the forest floor. To Bob's shock, his hand seized the landing skid on the other side and he flipped into the cockpit.

The machine guns stopped as the helicopter moved wildly. It lurched forward to the point the windshield faced the ground, its spinning blades perpendicular to the earth. The helicopter leveled off and Bob could barely see Director Veritably fighting against Charlie.

Bob said, "He's...brave." Anything more and he was going to be ill.

"Well said, Agent Bob. Stay down!"

The unmanned, unaimed machine guns fired again. The bullets launched up and down, left, and right, then in complete circles. One sailed so close to Bob's neck, the hairs on the back of his neck tingled.

Crunch! A stone column completely crumbled. Then the next stone and the next, going far off into the distance.

"Hang on!"

The motorcycle swerved left. *Crash!* Right. *Crash!* Chunks of tunnel collapsed much faster.

Boom! The left side of the tunnel caved in and threw them back into darkness. The sound of the stone hitting the floor sounded like fate taunting them, laughing at their futile efforts to flee. Agent Sol kept yelling to Bob, though he wasn't sure if it was to keep him positive or to lie to herself.

"I see light!" Agent Sol said. Bob didn't dare look.

She zigzagged through the tunnel, Bob squeezing tighter around her stomach each time. He suddenly felt weightless, until they slammed back to the ground. Tiny debris smacked against his back faster and faster. Suddenly, a torrent of very heavy raindrops that sounded much like the collapsing tunnel minutes earlier grew louder and screamed closer, the torrent only feet behind him. Gusts of air blasted him, thrown from the mass falling behind him.

Whoosh. The crumbling sound grew distant, and the engine's roar dulled, no longer contained by the stone walls. Agent Sol slowly stopped the bike.

"It's okay, Bob. You can open your eyes."

Bob eased his grip around her stomach and sat himself up, at last feeling safe under the embrace of the sun's warmth. His stomach was still roiling, but it was easier to breathe. Having two feet on stable ground in this short, grassy plain was a godsend.

Agent Sol was covered in dirt and black specks of debris so thick Bob couldn't see her skin or cable repairer uniform anymore, except for the part where Bob had wrapped his arms around her, which remained its original color. Even Bob was a bit dirty, though the front of him was mostly fine.

"Excellent work, Agent Sol," he said, stepping off the bike. "Sorry, I must've been poisoned by enemy—" After dry heaving for a moment, Bob focused only on his breathing. Agent Sol giggled.

"Yes, that must've been it. Glad to see the effects are wearing off," she said. Agent Sol got off the bike and faced the collapsing tunnel. Far beyond, fires blew out of the castle's windows and cracks erupted in the walls. The soft rumble of explosions continued like a song until the building collapsed in on itself.

Beneath the exploding castle were hundreds of people neatly exiting the service tunnel they had used to get into D.I.R.T. headquarters. Agent Dawn led them. She was calling out names through a microphone, one of which Bob recognized.

"Ned Lorox? Great. Let's get him in handcuffs," Agent Dawn said. Good to know that he made it out safely. It seemed like everything was all wrapped up. The base was blown up. The bad people were defeated. They completed the chase...

Bob shuddered. This was usually when the kiss scene happened, but he was not in shape for it. The kiss scene created another predicament because he really liked Agent Sol. Could he turn off real-life Bob and focus on how Agent Bob would handle the situation? He'd have to apologize for his poisonous gas breath afterward. Bob struggled to stand tall, then he walked toward Agent Sol so he could be in position if she initiated the kiss. But then, the man always initiates the kiss in action spy movies. But then, this was supposed to be a comedy, even though he had his doubts. Also, those movies were kind of old school, so given the modernness of the script and Charlie being the director, maybe Charlie wanted her to kiss Bob first. It was times like these he could really use a script.

Agent Sol didn't react like she was getting ready for a kiss. She just stared at the explosion, not turning her head to address Bob.

"You alright over there?" she said.

Bob gave a thumbs up, then remembered she wasn't looking at him. "Good," he said, struggling to hold back his tormented stomach. Given she still didn't turn around, Bob gladly sat down on the motorcycle. It made him feel a little better. There wasn't a kiss scene. He took a deep breath. The air was fresh, earthy, and gentle on his stomach.

Agent Sol headed back to Bob, patted him on the back, and said, "Cut. Good work today, Bob. Let's get you home."

Bob heard the helicopter before it appeared from behind the collapsed tunnel. It didn't fire, and Charlie didn't speak. When it landed by them, far enough away that the kicked-up rocks and loose grass didn't pelt them, Bob squinted and saw Director Veritably in the pilot's seat. The helicopter powered down, and Director Veritably stepped out.

"You both did excellent work," he said. "Bob Johnson, you went above and beyond the call of a normal agent—"

"Actor, sir. The scene is over," Agent Sol said.

"Yes, sorry, I meant actor. Bob, you improvised like a professional...Lila Sol, when I recruited you five years ago, I knew you had promise, but your performance today blew away all my expectations in the best way possible. I hope you continue serving the film industry and the world the same way you did today."

Agent Sol gave a professional nod, but Bob spotted a sly smirk.

"Now, agents—actors," Veritably said, then muttered something in a frustrated voice, "let's get you home." He waved for them to join him in the helicopter. Bob hesitantly boarded but then felt Agent Sol's comforting hand on his back.

"Come on, Bob. Only a little farther," she said. She smiled softly when Bob looked at her. He faced forward to hide his blush.

"Hurry up, you two," Director Veritably said, getting in his seat. He flipped a bunch of switches, and the helicopter whirled to life. Agent Sol handed Bob a headset, then put one on herself. She confirmed they were set, and the helicopter lifted into the air.

Bob looked backward to find a bound and gagged Charles, as well as another D.I.R.T. actor. "Are they supposed to be like that?" Bob said.

Director Veritably said, "They betrayed the studio, Bob. We take that *very* seriously."

Bob gulped. There was a vengeful fire in Charlie's stare. Bob just faced forward and closed his eyes. He told himself again and again that it was almost over until he fell asleep.

Bob took a seat in Veritably's office. It was surprisingly untouched given the rest of the C.L.E.A.N. set was a mess. On his way to the office, Bob passed dozens of black suit actors scrubbing the walls with brushes to get the marinara off or patching the walls to fix the wine craters. Others were bent over buckets and scrubbing clothes to get the stains out. Occasionally, they would look up at Bob and give him a cheer. Whoever was in charge now must've decided to save some money and have the actors clean up the set for another scene or movie.

After they reached his office, Director Veritably spun around in his chair. He pulled some folders from his desk and laid out a row of papers.

"Bob," he said, "you came here as an extra and are potentially leaving as an actor. First, let's discuss your compensation." Director Veritably slid forward the leftmost paper.

Bob's eyes jumped out of his head. He looked up from the number in disbelief. There were too many zeroes for Bob to count. Veritably nodded approvingly and snickered.

"The studio," he said, "is paying you for your performance as well as your silence. It's vital to this nation's—this studio's security that you do not say anything about what you saw or did today. This second paper is an offer of employment. If you want to join our operations." Director Veritably slid the second paper forward.

Bob bit his lip and stared at the offer with wide excited eyes. He would become an actor. Well, the contract had the word agent written, but someone crossed it out and wrote *actor*. It was probably another cost-saving measure to reuse a prop contract instead of drafting a real one. TV actors had it rough. There were so many extremes, and it was so unpredictable and...Bob took a deep breath and hoped he wouldn't regret his next move.

"Thank you, but after today, I really don't think I want to be an actor. It was really for money, which you guys definitely gave me, and to get my parents into a yacht club, but my friends are going to help with that. So..."

Veritably leaned back in his chair and chuckled. He crossed his arms.

"I got to admit that threw me for a bit of a surprise. Maybe it's good I'm retiring. Not as sharp as I used to be. Well, wherever you end up is lucky to have you. So, that means we need this third form." He scooted back up to the desk and rested his arms on it. He slid it in front of Bob.

It was a long, multi-page document with very tiny font like a swarm of ants on a page. Bob skimmed over it and saw lots of mentions of *federal government* and *treason* and even *executed* a couple of times. He nervously raised his eyes up to Veritably, who anticipated the question.

"I understand your concern. That's a lot of legal jargon. But it's fine!" He gave a dismissive wave. "Just don't talk about the movie with anyone, unless otherwise authorized by me or Agent Sol or if you see something released online by the federal government, and you'll live a long and happy life."

Bob gulped and confidently signed the third form. Veritably stood from his desk, and they shook hands.

"Take care, Bob."

"You too, Veritably. Enjoy your retirement."

Bob headed out but stopped in the doorway.

"Also, Charlie is a good guy. I know he may have messed up, but he made a mistake and got caught up. If you give him a chance, he'll make things right."

Veritably just gave a nod and Bob continued out of the office. Lila was standing right outside the door, leaning against the wall.

"You really are something else," she said. "After all that, you don't want to become an actor?"

Bob shrugged his shoulders.

"Yeah, I'm sorry. It was right before we shot that arena rescue scene. Being one of you might've been cool, but if this is what TV comedy takes, it just doesn't seem like it's for me."

"Fair enough," she said with a stifled smile. "Let's get you home."

They walked back to the vehicle hangar where a black limo waited for them, surrounded by toppled and destroyed vehicles and dozens of black suit actors cleaning up the wreckage. They stopped and cheered Bob and Lila as they got into the limo. Myers, the guy who snagged Bob way earlier in the day, was cheering louder than anyone else.

The limo's windows were fully black, so Bob couldn't see outside, and soundproof, so the cheers from the outside faded instantly once Lila closed the door. He didn't really notice because he was talking with her the whole time.

Before Bob realized it, the limo slowed to a stop and the doors unlocked.

"Well, here's your stop," Lila said. They scooted out of the limo and stood on the sidewalk outside Bob's apartment. She wore jeans and a tank top with a picture of donuts on it, and Bob wore the clothes he started the day in, washed personally by Veritably after Director and Linda McCarthy returned them.

Under a bright moon and in the cool evening air they strolled to his front door. Lila, looking nothing like her character now, stopped as Bob climbed the stoop. He stared at the doorknob.

A thousand scenarios played out in his head. He knew what he wanted to ask, but he also knew that she said she would let him know. Bob didn't want to press it, but he knew he'd regret it if he didn't ask again. They probably wouldn't see each other, so if there was any awkwardness, at least they'd both forget it eventually. They could be friends even if Bob wasn't getting into acting. Okay, he'd ask for her number and not a date. If she wanted to go on a date, she could bring it up. If she didn't, they could just stay friends. Bob sighed. He had stared at the knob for at least thirty seconds, and she had probably walked away by now.

However, when he turned to check, she stood there smiling, hands folded in front of her. Bob poorly hid his surprise and awkwardly played off his small jump.

"Oh, you're still here. Um...please say no if you're not into it or if it's not professional and stuff, but, like, do you mind if I ask for your number? It's only so, like, if I get back into acting, I can ask for advice and stuff since you're, like, doing this, and you're amazing and—"

"Bob..."

"Oh, right, yeah, I'm sorry for pressing it. It's just that —"

"Bob!"

She gestured for his phone and typed in her number and a nickname. *Ly.* She stepped forward, kissed him on the cheek, and started walking back to the limo. "I'd like to go on a date with you. Text me tomorrow, okay? Have fun with your friends." With a flick of her hand, Bob's friends burst from a nearby alley.

Moni got to him first, but they all barraged him with questions. Bob was frozen still watching Lila vanish into the limo and disappearing into the night.

Bob eventually snapped out of it, and they all went out that night. He tried inviting Ned and Charlie, but to Moni's disappointment they didn't answer their phones. Veritably's haunting words echoed in Bob's head...*They betrayed the studio.*

Eventually, midnight rolled around, and Bob returned to his studio apartment. He tripped on a few pieces of exercise equipment, then crashed onto his bed. Right before he fell asleep, Bob made a note to clean up.

Epilogue

"There's nothing to be nervous about, Ly," Bob said to Lila seated next to him in the back of a taxi with sticky seats that wreaked of sweat—mostly his. The two were meeting his parents at the yacht club. Today was his parents' induction ceremony, and an excellent time to introduce Lila to them. "Sure, you are the first woman I've ever introduced to my parents, and they are super judgmental and were super mad at me for not being an actor despite our TV show-turned-movie being a box office success and—"

"Bob," Lila said with a playful slap to his thigh, "there's nothing to be nervous about. I've dealt with people much more intimidating than your parents and it went wonderfully."

She was right as always. As his mind calmed a bit, Bob reached for her hand, gave it a quick squeeze, and smiled back at her.

The cab came to a stop at the roundabout in front of a covered entrance. Weathered white wooden stairs rose to a landing, beyond which were two crystal-clear glass doors, both labeled *Still Rivers* in overly elaborate cursive.

They got out of the cab. Bob re-buttoned his navy-blue suit and smoothed out the flaps that bunched while they were sitting in the cab. He extended a hand to Lila, whose beige dress with navy-blue sash around her waist shimmered under the noon sun. As Bob and Lila entered the building, two men standing by the doors, dressed in red vests, white shirts, and black pants, opened the doors and bowed their heads.

Bob and Lila walked through the nautical theme and regal lobby to the outer deck that looked over the docks and a massive river, beyond which lay Central City washed over in a haze from the distance. Yachts with multiple levels and decks filled the background, some with sails and some without. On one of the smaller boats, still massive by any normal standard, were his parents. His mom waved to Bob. Bob knew her well enough to know that she wanted to yell and get his attention, but after becoming part of 'high society,' she tempered herself when she was around this crowd.

Bob gave a quick exhale and wiped the sweat from his forehead. There were a thousand ways for this to go wrong. Lila reached for his hand, and they intertwined fingers.

"It's going to be fine," she said.

Bob wished she would record that into a button that he could press constantly.

His mom pointed up to the observation deck above them, which Bob and Lila reached by climbing a spiral staircase tucked in the corner of the deck.

The observation deck looked identical to the one below, just without the stairs or a level above it. Two differences were the fully stocked wooden bar that Bob noted for later and a mini stage opposite the staircase that held an ornate sea-themed podium. The wood was weathered, and the four corners were in the shape of masts.

Bob scanned the seating chart by the stairs for the names of those at his table. It was his family, Lila, and the Loroxes.

"Hey! Ned and Charlie are coming too. Awesome," Bob said.

Lila's normally calm face cracked a bit at the mention of Charlie. Bob continued.

"I know he was a bad director, and he betrayed the studio, but he's still my friend. He's a good guy."

"Let's get our seats." Lila dragged Bob along. His parents arrived a few minutes later and sat too.

"Mr. and Mrs. Johnson! Nice to meet you both," Lila said. "Bob has told me so much about you."

"Oh, please sit! No need to get up. Bob also told us so much about you!" his mom said. His dad just gave an agreeing head nod.

"Has he now?" Lila said.

"Oh, yes. Only good things, don't you worry!" His mom gave a playful flick of the wrist.

There wasn't a moment Bob wasn't stuffing his mouth with food. If it was full, he couldn't say anything stupid. Bob tried to remember what he told his mom. It wasn't how they met or anything. Mainly things that happened during their dates and—Bob stopped chewing.

Last week, when Bob asked his mom if Lila could attend the dinner, he foolishly let it slip. The L word. Both his parents teased him. It was the first time he told his parents he felt that way about someone. He had to derail the conversation. Bob hadn't said the L word to Lila yet, and now wasn't when he was going to do it. Then, he was saved by the grace of well-timed interruptions.

"Leave some for us!" someone said. Bob recognized Mr. Lorox coming up to the table, with Mrs. Lorox, Ned, and Charlie tailing behind. The men wore tan, blue, and gray suits. Mrs. Lorox wore a sequined gray dress that reached to right above her ankles.

They all took a seat and joined right in on the conversation. It started off with the basics. Congratulations on getting in. Thanks for the recommendation. How are you doing? What's been going on? Then his mom, Mr. Lorox, and Mrs. Lorox, got into the gossip.

"Oh, so you didn't have any issues with your appliances?" his mom said. Mr. Lorox shook his head and shrugged his shoulders.

"Not a one!" he said. "It was the weirdest thing. Our neighbors texted us and said they had the same issues you guys had." Lila, Ned, and Charlie quickly chewed and swallowed whatever they had in their mouths.

"Oh, but that was just marketing for the movie, right? I don't think we need to talk about that anymore," Ned said.

"Yeah, Ned's right," Charlie said. "It was a cheap Hollywood stunt."

"Capitalism! Gurr!" Lila said.

Bob shrugged his shoulders. There definitely was a massive marketing campaign the day after Bob finished filming.

The conversation then moved on to Mr. Lorox and Bob's mom commenting on other people's outfits. Bob fully tuned out of that. So did his dad, who talked with Ned about car stuff. Another uninteresting topic. Bob turned to Lila and Charlie, but they silently stared at each other. Lila looked like she wanted to attack Charlie, and Charlie looked like a wounded puppy.

"Hey, Charlie," Bob said, "how are things going?"

Lila backed off a little but didn't fully turn off her stare. Charlie stuttered for a bit then turned to Bob.

"Oh, working on things here and there. I did want to thank you for going to bat for me with Veritably. Everything you said during...the last time we saw each other...got to me. I was lost in the sauce." He chuckled nervously as Lila reached for her butterknife, which she could turn into a weapon. Bob discreetly snatched her hand under the guise of romance and pulled it under the table. Charlie still looked nervous.

"Yeah, so I started helping the community and getting back to what made me happy when I was younger," Charlie said.

"That's awesome! Where are you working? Boy Scouts? St. Michael's food drive? Boys and Girls Club?" Bob said.

Charlie leaned forward and put his elbows on the table. "Not exactly. More stopping criminals."

"Charles Richard Lorox," Mrs. Lorox said in a seething whisper, "how many times do I have to tell you to not put your elbows on the table?"

"Sorry, Mom," he said. Charlie quickly corrected his posture then got back to a whisper. "I was actually hoping you could help me."

Bob shrugged and turned to Lila, who didn't take her eyes off Charlie. He turned back to his friend and said, "Like working with the police? That kinda sounds fun."

"Yeah, kind of like working with the police. I feel like you could be really good at it."

"Thanks. I'm only working part-time at Merlin's Designer Warehouse, so I do have some free time. Plus, it'll be good to get active and stuff. I haven't been doing my stunt and gym training as much anymore. So, yeah! Let me know the next time you go."

"Definitely." Charlie smiled and leaned back.

Sometime after that, a mountain of a man came up the stairs. Each one of his steps shook the observation deck. Bob's table fell silent as the man walked behind the podium. He was so massive Bob almost didn't notice the woman walking beside him.

The man rested his tree trunk arms on the podium and adjusted the microphone. He had no facial hair and a bowl-cut hairstyle that framed his blunt features, dark black eyes, and forehead wrinkles. He wore a very loud Hawaiian shirt and a gold watch that sent a glare into Bob's eyes.

The woman next to him was younger, with long red hair running like a river along the side of her face, over her bare shoulders, and down to her ruby-colored dress, with a low cut and exposed back.

The man tapped the microphone. "Welcome, everyone, to the 15th induction ceremony of the Still Rivers Yacht Club sponsored by Raghu Food Distribution. For those who don't know, I am the president of this wonderful organization, Reginald Raghu. This wonderful person standing next to me, Sarah Crafterson, serves as our vice president."

Bob grew bored as Reginald verbally patted himself on the back and thanked a bunch of other people. Other tables were laughing, so Bob figured there were a bunch of inside jokes he didn't understand or care about. His parents were laughing but clearly didn't understand what was going on either since their laughs always started after everyone else's like an echo.

He turned to Lila, who gave him an eye roll, like *This is ridiculous*, then snapped to proper form when Bob's mom turned to her.

Bob's attention then turned to Charlie, who now looked like a lion preparing to strike.

"*Psst*," Bob said. "Charlie, you okay?"

Charlie turned back, and his attacking aura disappeared. Charlie leaned forward and whispered to Bob. "Yeah. You remember that thing I told you I was getting into? He's my first target—the kingpin of it all."

About the Author

When not writing reports or hanging with friends and loved ones, P.J. Cruz writes books about wannabe actors, wannabe superheroes, and everything in between. His books haven't won any awards just yet, but he'd be happy and grateful to have you join his ride to the top.

P.J. Cruz has been writing since he was a kid though he took a break during college, during which he earned his Bachelors in Economics and Juris Doctor from the University of Florida. After that, he returned home to the Jersey Shore and writes any chance he gets.

instagram.com/AuthorPjCruz

amazon.com/P-J-Cruz/e/B0BTVC7M94/ref=aufs_dp_fta_dsk

tiktok.com/@authorpjcruz

Also by P.J. Cruz

Bob lives a quiet life in Central City. His days are routine, but he always enjoys lunches from his local restaurants. Then, one day his favorite sandwich is replaced with a culinary abomination. Bob quickly learns that a dark and flavorless shadow is sweeping over the city. A money hungry villain and his army of thugs slowly take over the city, one store at a time after which it is left only with terrible food to serve. Now, Bob must team up with his friends to save the city or be doomed to eat terrible food for the rest of his life. Will Bob save the sandwiches or get lost in the sauce?

Available on Amazon Now